A HUNTER'S REVENGE

When Jim Harding, a bounty hunter who had tired of his profession, arrives in Sentenas, he expects his brother to be waiting for him at the station. Instead, he finds him hanging from a rope in the barn adjoining the ranch they had bought together a few weeks earlier. His brother's murder, two ambushes and the kidnapping of the woman he wants to marry, lead Harding back into the kind of action he had desperately wanted to leave behind . . .

KENT MASTERS

A HUNTER'S REVENGE

Complete and Unabridged

LINFORD
Leicester

First published in Great Britain in 1993 by
Robert Hale Limited
London

First Linford Edition
published 2001
by arrangement with
Robert Hale Limited
London

British Library CIP Data

Masters, Kent
  A hunter's revenge.—Large print ed.—
Linford western library
1. Western stories
2. Large type books
I. Title
823.9′14 [F]

ISBN 0–7089–9702–3

WES
1321156

Published by
F. A. Thorpe (Publishing)
Anstey, Leicestershire

Set by Words & Graphics Ltd.
Anstey, Leicestershire
Printed and bound in Great Britain by
T. J. International Ltd., Padstow, Cornwall

This book is printed on acid-free paper

1

It had surprised Jim Harding when his brother had not met him off the train. Surprise had turned to anxiety when there had been no trace of him when he had arrived at the ranch. That had been thirty-six hours ago. Now he was very worried.

Harding took off his hat and wiped the sweat from his forehead. Since early morning, he'd been fencing in the property he'd bought with his brother two weeks earlier and his body was already beginning to ache at the continuous efforts demanded of it. He screwed up his eyes against the glare of the midday sun. Shielding them with his hat, he watched as a cloud of dust approached him through the ravine a few hundred yards away. He grunted. Now Jess would have some explaining to do.

Gradually, the silence of the range that had pressed in on him only minutes earlier was broken by the thundering sound of horses' hooves. He stiffened. It wasn't Jess. He reached out and picked up the gun belt he'd discarded whilst linking his posts with gleaming bob wire and buckled it around his waist.

The two horsemen reined in sharply, cursing loudly when they saw the wire that barred their path and the lone man standing behind it.

'What the hell is all this?' one of them demanded angrily, trying to control his nervous horse. He was a very tall, thin man with watery blue eyes hidden beneath shaggy black eyebrows. 'Who gave you the right to string this wire across open trail?'

'There's no trail here,' replied Harding. 'This is my land.'

'What!' the man shouted. 'Who the hell are you?'

'The name's Jim Harding and this is my northern boundary.' He shrugged his wide shoulders to ease his stiff and aching muscles. 'I've fenced this off to stop my cattle straying into the ravine,' he continued, nodding towards the distance.

'I'm Carl Jenkins,' the beanpole said angrily. 'My ranch is due north of here. I use this trail to town every week. If I didn't, it'd mean an extra ten miles on my journey. And I also use that water-hole at your back for my horses.' He nodded past Harding, then turned in the saddle to face the man beside him. 'Ritter, tear this damn wire down.'

Harding looked hard at the man Jenkins had just addressed. His face seemed vaguely familiar and the mention of his name jogged Harding's memory. The lean, cruel face that grinned back at him had stared out of many wanted posters Harding had seen before leaving Missouri.

'This is not free range, Jenkins,' snapped Harding. 'You've no right to cross my land without my say so.' He nodded at the fence he'd just erected.

'That's to protect my stock and it'll stay there as long as I want it to. And the water-hole you've had easy access to in the past is also mine.'

'You heard me, Ritter,' Jenkins snarled. 'Get his cutters and open this fence up.'

Ritter smiled maliciously as he swung down off his horse.

Harding's lips tightened. He watched grimly as Ritter swaggered across to the cutters lying on the ground. He sighed inwardly. So there was no escape.

He had left the wild, open plains of Missouri and laid down his gun after twelve years of bounty hunting. From a raw, gun-toting youngster, he'd become a keen-eyed, fast shooting man who'd never lost a gunfight. But he'd begun to notice the erosion the passage of time had caused. He no longer had the razor-sharp reactions of his twenties and had decided to hang up his guns before he found himself looking at death through the barrel of one gun too many. The invitation from his brother

Jess to join him in Texas as his partner in running a spread had finally made up his mind.

So he had finished with the bloody violence that had scarred his life for the previous twelve years. Some had said that he'd lost his nerve. That he'd turned yellow and was running away. They hadn't remembered all the killers he had corralled. Killers no lawman would chase. He had served the community, in his own way, but those who had taunted him chose to forget that. He'd shrugged his shoulders and ignored the taunts. He hadn't turned chicken. He had simply tired of the constant violence that had begun to blight his life.

And, having spent so many nights alone on the trail, listening to nothing but coyotes howling, he had grown lonely and hankered after finding himself a woman and settling down. He'd known that he'd never be able to do that as long as he carried a gun in anger.

But now he was beginning to think that there was no escape from the badmen. 'What makes you think you've got a right of way across my land?' Harding asked quietly. It was just possible Jenkins did have a legitimate reason for crossing his land. If he did, he'd listen to him. If bloodshed could be avoided, that had to be for the best.

Jenkins glanced at him suspiciously. 'This is the quickest way to Sentenas. If I go around them hills, it'll add an hour on to my journey. And my horse needs water on the way.'

Harding nodded. 'You been using this trail long?'

'Sure have,' said Jenkins, his eyes glinting.

'Well, I'm a reasonable man. The fence stays, to prevent my stock from straying, but I'll let you put a gate in it. And you can use the water-hole whenever you want to.' Wherever Jess was, Harding figured that he wouldn't mind him making this small concession to avoid trouble.

Jenkins grinned. 'That's real neighbourly of you.' Then his face hardened. 'How am I going to get through now?'

'I'll cut the top two strands and you can jump over,' replied Harding.

'Now why didn't I think of that?' said Jenkins, grinning again.

Harding picked up his cutters and carefully snipped the top two strands, protecting his face from the wire that whipped and twanged viciously the moment he cut it. 'That'll let you through.'

'I'll remember this,' said Jenkins. He turned to Ritter. 'Mount up. Let's go.'

Ritter scowled at Harding before he swung back into the saddle, his hard, dark eyes glittering with danger. Harding could see that he was itching for trouble. He had seen that look in many men's eyes during his time. It was the kind of naked desire to kill that he thought he'd left behind.

Harding was in thoughtful mood as he watched them ride away. He got down to repairing his fence, deciding that he'd put a gate in the next day. By then, maybe Jess would be back to give him a hand. Right now, he was too tired and wanted to have a couple of cups of strong coffee and something to eat.

But the thought of the two men he had just encountered worried him. He figured they were trouble. And that was the last thing he was looking for. He believed he had done the right thing in not provoking a fight. But he knew that he couldn't let them ride roughshod over him any time they felt like it. He wanted to be neighbourly. But he also had to stand up for his own rights if they were threatened. Then the gnawing in his gut returned as he suddenly remembered the unexplained absence of his brother.

He packed up his tools and was about to ride back to his shack when he noticed another cloud of dust in the distance. 'Looks like they're heading in my direction as well,' he mused. 'Sure is getting busy around here.' Slowly easing his Winchester out of its greased leather case, he let it hang loosely in his arms as the cloud of dust slowly approached him.

Three riders reined in beside the fence. They looked at Harding, their blank expressions betraying no emotion. The one in the middle, a small, fat man with ruddy cheeks and thinning grey hair spoke. 'I understand you're the new owner of this spread.'

Harding nodded. 'Along with my brother.'

'Haven't met either of you so me and the boys thought we'd come round and welcome you.' He jerked his head in the direction they had just come from. 'I own the Double Horn, west of you. My name's Johnson. This is my son, Pete,' he continued, indicating the thin young man at his right hand, 'and my foreman, Bret Carver.'

Harding introduced himself. 'You want some coffee?' he asked. 'I was just about to go back to the shack and make myself some.'

'Thanks,' Johnson replied.

Harding looked carefully at him. Although at first sight Johnson looked a rather careworn and lazy man, Harding saw a steady determination in his grey-blue eyes. This is a man I could trust, Harding thought instinctively. A good man to have as a neighbour.

'I know how much work is involved in getting a ranch into working order,' said Johnson. 'One of the reasons we came over was to see if you wanted any help.'

'That's real kind of you,' replied Harding. 'But I think I've got everything under control at the moment.'

Bret Carver looked sharply at Johnson. 'Just tell him! I don't like all this messing around.'

'You never did learn any social graces, did you, Bret?' Johnson's voice held a hint of sarcasm. 'But I guess you do have a point. We have more than enough work of our own to be getting on with.' Johnson looked directly at Harding. 'I pride myself on figuring out what kind of man I talk to . . . and I

10

reckon you're a good 'un.' He paused, still gazing directly at Harding. 'Time will prove me right or wrong, but for the time being, I reckon you're a man I can trust and maybe even be friends with. That's why I'm telling you to be real careful about your neighbour to the north, feller by the name of . . . '

'Jenkins,' interrupted Harding.

A look of surprise flitted across Johnson's face. 'You've met him already?'

'He rode through here just a couple of minutes before you.'

'What did he say about you putting up this fence?' asked Carver. 'Bet he wasn't too pleased about it.'

Harding gave a grim smile. 'You're right. He said he used this trail to get to Sentenas and more or less told me he was pulling it down.'

'So how come it's still standing? That feller usually gets his own way around these parts,' said Johnson.

'Only because of that hired killer of his,' snorted Carver.

'Ritter?' enquired Harding.

'That's him. A real mean killer,' said Carver.

'I got the impression he was itching to start some trouble when he and his boss showed up.'

'So how come you've still got wire across here?' asked Johnson again.

Harding explained to them what had happened. As he listened, Johnson gave a low whistle under his breath and shook his head slowly. 'I'm real surprised that they didn't give you more trouble,' he murmured. 'You must have caught Jenkins on a good day.'

Twenty minutes later, they were all sitting in Harding's shack with steaming mugs of coffee in their hands. 'You want something to eat?' asked Harding.

'No thanks,' replied Johnson. 'We ate before we came out.' His face was creased in a frown.

'Something bothering you?' asked Harding.

Johnson drained his mug and stared

straight at Harding. 'You be on your guard against Jenkins and his killers. They're real bad trouble.'

Carver thumped his fist into the palm of his left hand. 'We've been losing cattle for over a year from our ranch. We can't prove that Jenkins is taking them but I'm sure him and his bunch are rustling . . . and we're not the only ranch suffering in these parts.'

Johnson nodded his head vigorously. 'You're going to get trouble from that bunch before long,' he said.

Harding played with his mug of coffee. This was the kind of news he didn't want to hear, especially with his brother missing. Despite all his hopes, he hadn't left trouble behind him in Missouri. But he wouldn't run from it. He had to make a stand because he had no intention of giving up the ranch. 'Thanks,' he muttered. 'I'll look out for them.'

His concern for Jess was now at fever pitch. But he decided not to mention anything to Johnson. He'd wait just one more day and then go and see the sheriff.

'I guess you did the right thing in agreeing to put a gate in the fence,' said Johnson. 'At least you stopped them from giving you trouble right away. But they're going to leave that gate open every time they use it. They're not going to care if your cattle stray and get lost.'

'I appreciate you coming over and telling me all this. If there's anything I can do for you, just let me know,' said Harding.

'You're welcome over at my place any time,' said Johnson. 'The way you're starting up reminds me of when I did exactly the same thing. It's hard work, but it's worth it.' He stood up. 'Come over on a visit soon and I'll introduce you to my wife and daughter.'

After they had gone, Harding had another cup of coffee. He felt a strange comfort that Johnson was his neighbour but his forehead creased with a frown as he thought of the implications of

Johnson's warning. Violence was the last thing he wanted. But if it came looking for him . . . he shrugged his shoulders wearily. It looked as if it had already sought him out.

After another few hours' work, he returned to the shack. He lit a lamp as the sun began to dip below the horizon. The exertions of the day had tired him and his movements were laboured as he prepared himself a meal. Another strong cup of coffee revived him slightly and as he lay on his bunk, after having eaten his fill, he felt the contentment of a man who had laboured hard and done a good day's work.

He extinguished the lamp as he felt the long fingers of sleep clawing at him. Minutes later, he was plunging into a deep, satisfying chasm of darkness when a distant rumbling and hammering forced itself into his world. At first, he couldn't understand what had woken him up.

Suddenly, a bullet smashed through one of the windows and hammered into the wall above his head, spitting sharp splinters of wood all over him. Another followed, cannoned off the iron stove with a shriek of protest and whined into the wall.

Harding threw himself to the floor, all thought of fatigue and sleep forgotten. He grabbed his Colt from the holster hanging on the bedpost and rolled towards the door. Another volley of shots rang out, smashing into the shack. Splinters of wood and broken glass showered the floor.

Harding leapt to his feet and glanced quickly out of one of the smashed windows. He could see nothing in the darkness that enveloped the ranch. Then, the flash of a gun, as another shot thundered into the shack, gave him a clear indication of where his bush-whacker was staked out. 'Behind the rock on the left,' he muttered. 'I'll soon flush you out,' he added, gritting his teeth.

He waited. When the shots that thudded into the shack ceased, he flung the door open and hurled himself through it into the dirt. He lay flat on the ground, hugging it for cover and protection and waited. Another shot whined close to his head and another kicked up dirt beside him. Harding gritted his teeth again. He lay still until his unseen assailant had emptied his rifle, then jumped to his feet, anger coursing through him.

As he ran forward, firing at the boulder behind which the man had been sheltering, he heard the thunder of hooves as a horse galloped away into the night.

He sat down, a coldness settling on him. He felt a dryness in his mouth and his right hand, still clutching the Colt, trembled slightly.

He knew that he no longer had the sharpness and speed of a rattlesnake. He was getting old. At thirty-five, he was already an old man. Tonight's events had proved that. Back in his younger days, he'd have reacted far quicker than he had tonight. He'd have weighed up the situation, gone out the back door, waited for the flash from the rifle to help him identify where the bushwhacker was hiding, circled around behind him and brought him down.

But no more. Not only were his reflexes slower, his mind was no longer as agile and sharp as it used to be. He hauled himself wearily to his feet. A blanket of tiredness cloaked him again. He gazed at the darkness into which the man had ridden, sighed, then walked slowly back to the shack.

He didn't even attempt to clear up the mess caused by the ambush. He'd leave that till the following morning. He picked up his blankets, pulled them around him and lay down on the bed.

He reckoned that whoever had attempted to ambush him had not wanted to kill him. If he had, he could easily have done so. This had been a warning. But what for? Possibly to get him and Jess off the ranch. But who was responsible? And where was Jess?

Harding closed his eyes. Images of Ritter and Jenkins filled his mind. They gnawed away at him until, exhausted, he fell asleep again.

Warm beams from the early morning sun awoke him. Suddenly, remembering what had happened the previous night, he jumped out of bed and grabbed his gun. He surveyed the damage caused by the unknown gunman. He brewed some coffee, gulped it down, then started to clear up the mess. Using earth and clay he filled up the holes in the front of the shack caused by the powerful blasts from the gunman's rifle. When he had finished, he walked towards the boulder behind which the bushwhacker had sheltered. He found over a dozen spent cartridges and saw the tracks of the horse that had taken him to safety.

He thought of following them but quickly realized that the gunman would have laid a false trail. He'd never find him now. He returned to the shack and cooked himself some breakfast. After he'd finished eating, he headed for the barn.

As his eyes adjusted to the gloom, he saw a body swinging lazily from a beam. Whoever had tried to frighten him last night had left a message. A very clear message. Harding clenched his teeth.

Sick at heart and raging with anger, he buried his brother, sticking a rough hewn wooden cross into the freshly dug ground to identify his brother's final resting place.

He saddled up. Perhaps Jess had mentioned that his brother was a bounty hunter. Jess would have been easy to take. But they might have been reluctant to take on a bounty hunter, a man renowned for his fighting courage and skills.

Harding headed along the well-trodden trail which led to Sentenas. He needed to order some more bob wire and stock up with more provisions. Otherwise he'd run out of material to work with and food to keep body and soul together. But of far greater importance, he had to find his brother's murderers.

As he let the buckskin find its own way along the trail, Harding's thoughts returned to the events of the previous evening and that morning. They began to burn themselves into his mind. Suddenly, the crash of a rifle cracked through the still morning air.

Harding felt his hat being jerked from his head as if by an unseen hand. He spurred his horse on and raced towards the cover of some jagged rocks that lay just ahead of him. Three bullets splattered against a large boulder as he swung down from the saddle.

His face was taut and white with anger as he pulled his Colt out of its greased holster and peered around the rock. An angry whine as another bullet careered off the rock made him pull back his head. He flattened himself against the boulder, breathing heavily.

Whoever this was, he wasn't messing

about. The shots aimed at him were meant to hit their target. This hombre wasn't warning him off. He was deadly serious.

Harding crawled to the other side of the rock, then ran towards another, larger boulder and threw himself to the ground behind it. He wanted to get an idea of where the gunman was hiding. That way, he could plan his own response to this sudden and unexpected interruption to his journey.

Even as he hit the dirt, another bullet whacked into the ground beside him. Harding's mouth opened slightly, dismay and concern registering on his face. That last shot had come from a totally different place from the last one. There were two of them. Now he knew he had his work cut out. He'd have to draw on all his old reserves of cunning and skill to spring himself out of this ambush. A shudder of concern ran through him as he remembered his lacklustre reactions of the previous night. He wondered whether he could still manage it.

Further bullets hammered into the rock behind which he had taken cover, some whining their way into oblivion as they richocheted off the hard surface. He looked towards the buckskin. Perhaps the only way out was to jump on his horse, both Colts blasting at the areas in which the gunmen were hiding. If he rode out fast, that may be his best chance. He'd be a difficult target to hit.

But before he attempted to run back to the buckskin, he had to create a small diversion to draw the gunmen's fire. He grabbed a handful of small pebbles and threw them ten feet, behind some large boulders to his left, in the opposite direction to the way he was going to run.

As they landed in a cloud of dust, a hail of bullets thudded into the rocks around them. Harding scrambled into the open, heading towards the buckskin. Two bullets whacked into the ground a foot ahead of him, stopping him dead in his tracks. His mind froze, momentarily stunned with incredulity. A flash of fear twisted his face. There were three of them! He scrambled back to the cover of the rock, staring desperately at the buckskin. It was a well-planned ambush. Maybe the same type they had used for Jess. This time, they didn't mean to let him out alive.

2

Harding crawled closer to the rock that sheltered him from the spitting guns and rifles of the three men who were trying to kill him. He clenched his teeth and drew his lips back in a snarl of anger. He knew that his professed aim of leading a quiet, peaceful life was already in tatters. He had to fight. To forget all about the good intentions he'd had when he'd first set foot on this land. He growled deeply, rage surging through him. Another shot whined past him and spattered into the wall of rock at his back.

He rolled over to the edge of the boulder and loosed off a couple of shots at the area where he thought one of the gunmen was hiding. More shots cracked into the ground and boulders around him, throwing up puffs of dirt and causing splinters of rock to shower him as he clung to the hard stone for cover.

He quickly peered out to see if he could pinpoint where the shots were coming from. Before being forced to duck as more slugs came his way, he was able to see two small clouds of gunsmoke hovering in the still morning air, above well-protected rocks on the other side of the trail. 'That's two of them,' he muttered. 'Now where's the other one?'

Knowing that he was taking a calculated risk, Harding deliberately showed a glimpse of his head and shoulders to the other gunman who had stopped him dead in his tracks when he had run towards his horse. He had to get an accurate idea of where the man was holed up. Then he could decide whether to take evasive or direct action to get out of the corner he found himself in. He shut his mind to the possibility that the gunmen knew what he was up to and would change their positions deliberately to confuse him.

The second he showed himself, two bullets screamed towards him. But he had found out what he needed to know. He leant against the rock, waiting for the next volley of bullets. He figured that they would try and pin him down with heavy fire whilst one of them manoeuvred around to try and get a clear shot at him. But he also knew that when they emptied their guns, he'd have a chance to take a few well-directed shots back. If he managed to get one of them, the other two might lose heart and ride away. But he wasn't counting too much on that happening.

Suddenly, another burst of shots came whining towards him. Then, he saw a flash of colour darting between the rocks. They were trying to close in on him. He loosed off a shot at the flurry of movement, but the man was out of sight before it hammered into the dirt beside the rock he had flung himself behind.

Harding turned and looked out from

behind his boulder at the position of the other two gunmen. To his utter astonishment, he saw one of them out in the open, crouched low, moving towards him.

Harding fired two shots in quick succession. A terrible scream burst from the man's lips as the bullets tore through his bone and flesh. Harding watched with cold satisfaction as he crumpled to the ground, clawing at his shattered leg.

Harding had to take immediate cover as another shot splattered into the rock beside his head, throwing a cloud of dust into his face. He coughed and wiped his eyes with a rough, calloused hand. A ringing sound filled his head as another volley of shots crashed around him. The deafening noise was making his senses whirl.

But his ambushers were getting reckless and over confident. They thought they had him and were coming out into the open with a blatant disregard for their own safety. Perhaps they didn't realize who they were up against.

He saw the flash of a red shirt and an elbow poking out from behind another rock. He took careful aim and shot at the arm that was so carelessly exposed. He smiled coldly when he heard a cry of agony. Whoever it belonged to, Harding knew that the man's arm was now smashed and useless.

He took the opportunity created by his well-aimed shots to make a break for it. He had only run three yards when a bullet flashed past his head. Then he felt a searing hot pain tear through his right shoulder. He stumbled as his knees began to crumble beneath him. He twisted around to see where the shot had come from and saw a tall figure taking aim. In desperation, Harding swivelled round to face the man, raised his Colt and loosed off a shot. The man lowered his gun and darted behind a rock for cover. Harding staggered, then limped towards his buckskin, cursing at the agonizing pain that stabbed through his body.

He collapsed against a rock as more bullets from the rifle of the man who had darted for cover spat into the ground inches from his feet. He rolled on to his back, groaning at the sharp pain that seared through his shoulder.

He touched his shirt and felt a damp, sticky mess with his fingers. He was bleeding. He couldn't tell how badly but he knew one thing for sure. There was no way he could hold out until nightfall. Not in his present state. Once, when he was young and strong and quick as a rattlesnake, maybe. But not now.

He lifted his head, peering out to see if there was any further movement. No sooner had he done so than another bullet splattered into the rock inches from his face. He ducked, grimacing as another stab of pain shot through his shoulder.

He took comfort from the fact that only one of the gunmen appeared to be shooting at him now. The other two had been put out of action but there was no guarantee they'd stay that way, particularly the one he had injured in the leg. Harding smiled thinly, taking some satisfaction from the fact that he'd done some damage to at least two of them.

He reloaded his Colt with some bullets from his belt and spun the chamber around. He concentrated hard, listening for the smallest noise. If he heard them moving towards him, hoping for a kill, he'd get them in the open with a good chance of blasting them to hell and back.

But he heard nothing. An overwhelming silence blanketed the range. His wounded shoulder began to throb mercilessly. His head was pounding and the ground began to swim in front of his eyes. He knew he was growing weaker. A feeling of nausea grabbed at his throat. He swallowed hard. If he didn't staunch the flow of blood from his shoulder the gunmen wouldn't have to shoot him. He'd soon be dead anyway.

He swallowed again, his throat dry with the dust he had sucked in. Sweat dripped down the side of his face. Although he had left his shack in the early morning, the sun was now high in the sky and its powerful rays were already making him uncomfortably hot.

Water, he thought. He hadn't brought any with him because it wasn't that long a journey to Sentenas. 'I don't have a chance in hell without water,' he muttered grimly. He sat down on the hard-baked earth. He was fast running out of time and options and quickly came to the conclusion that there was nothing for it but to take them head on. He might blast his way out of their trap. He might not. But if he didn't, at least he would have the satisfaction of having gone down fighting and maybe taking some of them with him.

Hearing some movement behind him, he clutched his Colt tightly, crawled around to the other side of the rock and hauled himself up. He had no intention of being lured out into the open by one of their ploys. He was too old a hand at this game for that. When he judged the time was right, he'd make his move. But not before then.

Suddenly, his buckskin, which had waited quietly and patiently for him, despite all the shooting, snorted loudly. 'Whoa, boy,' Harding croaked through dried lips. 'It won't be long now.' It was as if the horse knew there was danger approaching and was trying to warn him. The horse snorted again and lifted its head, its eyes staring wildly at Harding.

But nothing happened. The silence was beginning to affect Harding almost as much as the bullets that had screamed their way towards him only minutes earlier. But he waited, with a patience born of long years of tracking and hunting down some of the most vicious killers in the Midwest.

'Drop that gun,' rasped a harsh voice. 'I've got you covered. If you try anything you'll get a slug between your shoulder blades.'

Harding gulped in astonishment. Whoever was behind him had to be an Indian, although the voice didn't bear this out. The gunman had crept up behind him without any sound and only a redskin had ever done that to Harding in all the long years he'd been hunting badmen.

He slowly tossed his gun away from him and lifted his hands, his face etched with pain as fire coursed through his shoulder. The gun clattered on the hard rock.

'Turn around . . . real slow,' the man ordered.

Harding turned to face the man who had crept up behind him so quietly, curious to see who had managed to take him by surprise. His eyes fixed on a tall, dark-haired stranger, and a slow whistle escaped his lips as he noticed the sheriff's star pinned on his black shirt.

Harding moistened his lips. 'I'm real pleased to see you, sheriff.'

The tall man, dressed all in black,

stood motionless, with his legs splayed wide, planted firmly on the ground. His Colt was trained directly at Harding's chest.

Harding started to walk towards him.

'Hold it.' The voice was commanding, although Harding noticed that it had lost its tense, rough edge.

The man in black nodded.

Harding continued. 'My brother's been murdered. I was bushwhacked last night. And this morning, on my way to town to report the murder, three men tried to ambush me.'

The tall man lowered his gun. 'My name's Turner. I'm the sheriff in these parts.' He slid his gun into its holster. 'Looks to me as if I came along at just the right time.'

Harding grinned. 'You sure did.'

Turner nodded. 'I heard some shots so I came over to investigate. Any idea who was responsible?' As he spoke, he threw Harding his can of water.

Harding shook his head. 'Nope. I've only met two of my neighbours, Jenkins

35

and Johnson, along with a couple of their side-kicks. I don't think they'd have bushwhacked me like this. Whoever it was, though, I shot two of them up pretty bad.'

'Jenkins, you say.' The sheriff's eyes narrowed.

'Yes.'

'There's been some rustling around these parts for quite a while and some folks think Jenkins and his posse of hired guns are behind it.'

Harding grimaced. 'I met one of them yesterday. Feller called Ritter.'

'He's a real nasty piece of work,' Turner said grimly. 'Do you think he might have anything to do with the trouble you've been having?'

'Maybe,' replied Harding. 'I certainly can't see Johnson having done anything like this. He seemed a real nice feller to me. Someone you could trust and be pleased to have as a neighbour.'

Turner grunted. 'What did you think of his foreman?'

'Carver?'

'Yes.'

Harding shrugged his shoulders. 'He was OK.'

The sheriff lit a smoke. 'Want one?'

'No thanks.'

Turner blew a cloud of blue smoke into the air before he spoke again. 'Carver gets a bit aggressive sometimes,' he said quietly.

'Why's that?'

Turner took another drag. 'His father and brother were taken in by a bounty hunter four years back. Only thing is, they were taken in dead. The bounty hunter still got his reward.' Turner eyed Harding calmly. 'The memory makes Carver go a bit crazy now and again. I understand the bounty hunter's name was Jim Harding.'

Harding's eyes grew steely cold. It seemed that there was no escaping his past. He suddenly recalled the son and father from Texas he'd taken in some years back. They'd robbed two banks, killing innocent people in the process and had a worthwhile price on their heads. And now he thought of it, they had been called Carver. He looked directly at the sheriff. 'You seem to know a lot about me.'

'That's my business,' replied Turner.

'I cornered them in a saloon,' Harding explained. 'You must know what it's like, being a lawman. The older man threw down his gun but the young feller took me on. Shot him straight between the eyes. The old man made a grab for the gun on the floor so I had no option but to shoot him as well.'

Turner nodded. 'No need to explain it to me. If you're going to explain it to anyone, it should be to Carver.' He pinched out his smoke. 'You mentioned you shot two of the hombres that ambushed you.'

Harding nodded, thoughts beginning to formulate in his mind that Carver might be responsible for Jess's murder and the attempt on his own life. Revenge for the killing of his father and brother.

'They've all probably hightailed it by now but best to have a look and see if they're still holed up anywhere,' said Turner.

They walked over to where Harding had shot the two bushwhackers. As expected, there was no sign of them, but some of the rocks and ground was spattered with blood. 'I hit them real good,' muttered Harding, taking some pleasure from that fact.

'Yeah. They'll be looking for someone to patch them up. I'll have a word with the doc when I get back to see if anyone's been to visit him.' He eyed Harding's shoulder carefully. 'You'd better get that seen to.'

Harding nodded, collected his buckskin, retrieved his hat and watched as the sheriff mounted his horse. 'What about my brother's murderers?'

'I'll make some enquiries when I get back to town. You just watch your back. You've upset somebody and I reckon they'll be after you again.'

Harding rode slowly into town and

headed straight for the doctor to have his shoulder patched up. He also wanted to find out if anybody had paid the doc a visit before he did, not wanting to wait until the sheriff got round to asking him. As expected, the doctor told him that he'd been his first customer that day.

An hour later, still nursing a painful shoulder, Harding walked to the store to order his provisions. Closing the door behind him, he blinked a couple of times to accustom his eyes to the gloom of the shop after the brilliance of the noonday sun. The first thing he noticed was the long flowing locks of a golden-haired woman standing beside the counter.

As if some instinct warned her of his intense gaze, the woman turned around. Their eyes locked. Her full red lips opened slightly and she gasped gently.

Harding felt a pounding in his chest that he had never experienced before. He had enjoyed many women. But the feelings he was experiencing at that moment were completely different to those he had felt in the past. Fire leapt between them as their eyes lingered on each other. Then she tore her gaze away from him as a blush stained her milky-white cheeks.

Harding knew that he wanted this woman. No matter what obstacles were placed in his way, he intended to have her. He walked towards her.

'Good morning, sir,' said the shopkeeper cheerfully. 'I'll be with you in a moment.' Having noticed the intensity of the brief glance between Harding and the woman he was serving, he continued, 'All ready for the wedding, are you Sarah? I must say, Sheriff Turner is a very lucky man.'

A searing stab of pain ripped through Harding at the shopkeeper's words. Yet another hammer blow delivered by the fates, attacking the plans he had begun to form just a few weeks ago. First, Jess's murder and the attacks on him, shattering the peace and solitude he had craved. Now, the seemingly insurmountable problem of the woman he knew he had to have being engaged to another.

'Ma'am,' he said quietly, 'please accept my good wishes for your forthcoming marriage. I've only been in these parts for a few days but I met your future husband on the trail this morning. I hope you'll both be very happy.'

'Thank you, Mr . . . '

'Jim Harding.'

'Thank you, Mr Harding.' He thought her eyes moistened with emotion as she spoke but he dismissed this as a wild dream on his part. He wanted her to feel the way he was feeling. But how could she? She was engaged to be married to another man. And even if he hadn't imagined her response, what then? No. The best thing he could do was to leave her life undisturbed. Yet the moment he had seen her, something inside him had told him that this was his woman. She was his destiny. He had to have her.

'Goodbye, Mr Harding. Nice to have met you.'

He watched her leave, then ordered his provisions. When he stepped out into the bright sunshine, he shielded his eyes to prevent himself from being blinded. Pulling his hat down low over his forehead, he decided to have a shot of whisky before heading home to do some more work on the spread.

He stepped off the boardwalk to cross the street to the saloon, hardly noticing the man coming towards him. His mind was still dwelling on Sarah's image. But a familiar, prickling sensation at the back of his neck alerted him to impending danger.

He looked at the man striding towards him. The man's eyes had a slightly crazed expression and his manner gave Harding the distinct impression that he was looking for trouble. It was Bret Carver.

3

'Just a minute, Harding. I want to talk to you.'

Harding braced himself for what he considered the inevitable clash between them. He saw Carver's right hand hovering uncomfortably close to the gun slung low on his hip. Suddenly, Carver raised his right arm as if to restrain Harding from walking past him. 'It won't take up too much of your time.'

Harding looked straight into Carver's strained and wide-open eyes, trying to determine when he'd make his move. 'What's on your mind?' he asked.

'Sheriff mentioned what happened to you last night and this morning when I saw him a couple of minutes ago.'

Harding nodded but said nothing.

'Some folk around here might think I was behind it.'

Harding remained silent. He felt it best to let the man talk. He figured that if Carver had been intent on a gunfight he wouldn't have bothered talking to him first. Perhaps he'd read him wrong.

'I wasn't. I know you shot my father and brother dead but I always knew they'd get what was coming to them. They were bad, real bad. And you were just doing your job . . . even if it was a job I don't respect much.'

A flicker of relief crossed Harding's features. He had enough troubles without Carver adding to them. He extended his hand and Carver shook it firmly. 'I'm glad you see it that way. When the sheriff told me about you I thought there might be trouble between us.'

'I'm a peaceable man, Harding, unlike the rest of my family.'

Harding nodded. 'I had to kill them,' he said quietly. 'Your brother went for his gun and your father followed suit. They had already killed seven men and I wasn't about to take any chances.'

'I understand,' said Carver. 'If it hadn't been you, it would have been another bounty hunter or some lawman.' A shadow of pain crossed his face as he spoke. Then he gave a faint smile. 'I got married last year and my wife is expecting our first child. My first priority is to look after them. All that stuff about my father and brother is in the past and that's where I aim to keep it. I want no trouble.'

'You'll have none from me,' said Harding. 'Good luck.' He shook Carver's hand once again.

'Thanks,' replied Carver. 'See you around maybe.'

Harding watched Carver stride down the street. He believed Carver was telling the truth. But something nagged away at the back of his mind like a tooth that was beginning to go bad. He didn't know why Carver hadn't toted a gun along with his father and brother. But blood was thicker than water and, as the sheriff had pointed out, their violent death had affected Carver in a strange way. Harding's eyes narrowed. There was just the possibility, however remote, that Carver would seek revenge one day. At a time and place of his own choosing. Perhaps he had already started with Jess.

What troubled Harding now was the puzzle of who, if not Carver, was responsible for the events of the last twelve hours. The only other people he had met were Jenkins and Johnson. Were they trying to scare him off? Or trying to kill him? And why? Whoever they were and whatever the reason, Harding vowed to stand firm, fight for himself and his land and most important of all, find Jess's murderers and bring them to justice.

The sun was high in the sky when he rode back to his ranch, having spent an hour or so in Sentenas. Just a mile or two from the shack, he took off his hat and wiped some sweat from his forehead, then took a swig of some water from the flash he had bought in town. He winced as pain shot through his arm.

He wondered how best to protect himself and his property, something he was unaccustomed to as he had never owned anything of consequence before, except his horse and guns. Suddenly, he heard the crack of gunshots in the distance.

Shielding his eyes from the sun and trying to see what was happening half a mile or so in front of him, he saw a gathering cloud of dust approaching him. A lone rider was making his way, at some considerable speed, towards town. He doubted if the rider had seen him yet.

As the rider got closer, Harding could see that he was wearing a flame-red shirt. Whoever he is, it's about time he went to the barber, mused Harding, noticing the long, flowing hair that streamed out from under the man's hat as the horse raced towards him.

His eyes opened in astonishment when he realized that the rider was not a man. It was Sarah. His throat tightened. What was she doing out here in the middle of a gunfight? He reined in her horse and quietened it down. 'Whoa, boy. Easy.' He looked at Sarah's face. It was red and flushed and her eyes were bright. When she spoke she was very agitated.

'Please help us. Somebody ambushed us . . . Ken is fighting back . . . he told me to get to town for some help but I don't think he'll be able to hold out for much longer. Please go and help him,' she implored.

Harding saw that Sarah was extremely distressed. He hesitated for a moment, uncertain as to how he should react when confronted with a woman in her state of mind. Then, as if he had been kick-started into action, he spoke. 'Where exactly is he?'

'Back there,' Sarah said tearfully, turning round and pointing back down the trail. 'Behind that clump of rocks.' Another volley of bullets made her jump. A strangled cry escaped from her lips. She yanked on the reins and swung away from Harding, clearly intent on heading back to Turner.

Harding attempted to grab the reins but failed. 'Don't . . . ' he shouted, but he was too late. She had spurred her horse and galloped towards the sound of gunfire before he had a chance to restrain her. 'Damn.' He was angry at her for being so irresponsible and angry at himself for having failed to stop her heading straight back into such a dangerous situation.

He watched in astonishment as she galloped around a bend in the trail and out of sight. Foolish she certainly was but there was also a great deal of courage within her slight young body.

No doubt it was driven to a degree by desperation at the thought of the plight of the man she was going to marry. The man she appeared to love so dearly. The doubt that crept into Harding's mind was there because of the way their eyes had locked in the store. Perhaps it had been his imagination. But for the first time in his life, he knew that he had designs on a woman who would almost certainly be denied him.

He followed her trail, listening intently for more gunfire, torn between the desire to help her and a natural caution at storming into a trap laid by the men who had ambushed the sheriff. Suddenly, the silence was broken by Sarah's scream for help. A wild panic tore through him. He urged his horse forward, concern for his own safety suppressed by the desire to help Sarah.

The sight that greeted him as he rounded the rocks behind which Sarah had disappeared only moments earlier made him wince. Sarah had obviously fallen to her knees beside the prostrate body of the sheriff, desperately trying to determine if he was dead or alive. But she hadn't managed to examine or comfort him for long. She was now in the grip of a man who was holding her tightly as a human shield in front of him.

Harding attempted to swing behind

some rocks to prevent the man from seeing him, hoping to gain at least some element of surprise. But he was too late.

'I seen you, feller,' the man shouted at him, grabbing Sarah even closer to him. 'Don't you try anything or she gets it right here,' he said, pressing his gun against her temple. Then a bullet whined past Harding's ear and another cracked into the rock beside him. He half turned in his saddle and saw an evil smile spread across the face of a man he knew to be a killer. It was Ritter.

'Jenkins sure would like to be here to see you get a slug between your eyes,' he shouted at Harding. 'We'll get rid of you on the same day as that troublesome sheriff. You didn't get the message last night and you slunk away this morning but we've got you now.' He laughed.

Harding swung down off his horse. He knew now who had killed Jess. What he didn't know was why. And why they had tried to kill him and ambushed the sheriff. But that wasn't his immediate concern. Another bullet whacked into the rock, showering him with splinters of stone.

He had a quick glance at Sarah. Ritter was pulling her towards the cover of some rocks at the top of the ridge from which he had probably launched the ambush on the sheriff. Sarah was kicking and struggling, arms and legs flailing but to no avail. Ritter held her in an iron grip, dragging her behind him as he slowly made for cover.

Harding continued to watch Ritter, hoping for a moment's carelessness that would give him the chance to take a clear shot at him. But the man was no fool. He was too experienced to let anyone have a shot at him while he had a hostage as cover. He carefully shielded his own body with Sarah's, preventing Harding or anyone else who came up the trail from having even a remote chance of loosing off a shot at him.

Harding felt a surging anger within

him. 'Who the hell do they think they are?' he exploded. 'They're behaving like wild coyotes, with no respect for any man or for the law.' He checked his Colt and his Winchester. 'Let's see what they're made of.'

He loosed off a couple of shots at one of the men's position. He heard loud cursing then a volley of bullets in reply splattered against the rock and whined over his head. Harding grinned. Ritter and his cronies could dish out some punishment but they obviously didn't like getting it back.

Harding tethered his buckskin and peered over the rock to see whether Ritter or anybody else was making a move. Nothing stirred.

Harding zigzagged his way between the rocks to get a better view of their positions, holding his wounded arm to protect it. As he did so, bullets started crashing into the ground around him, throwing up dirt by his feet. He dived for cover, both his guns spitting lead.

'They're not going to have it all their

own way,' he muttered grimly. Within seconds, he had reloaded and was pumping off more shots at their positions. He heard more loud cursing, then one man stood up and started emptying both guns at him. Harding smiled thinly. He counted the shots. Then he leapt out from behind the cover of the rocks and blasted away three shots.

A loud scream came from the bloodless lips of the gunman as he was thrown back into the dirt. He was dead before his body thudded to the ground.

Harding immediately sought fresh cover, darting between the rocks, seeking a more advantageous position to launch more attacks. His thoughts were constantly on Sarah's plight. That was why he was here. It seemed that both their fortunes were now tied together.

As Harding darted between the rocks, trying to get a better vantage point to attack, he saw the prone body of Sheriff Turner twenty yards in front of him, legs spreadeagled and face down. Harding blinked, then wiped some sweat from his brow. He saw two dark patches of blood on the sheriff's back. He feared that there was nothing he nor anybody else could do for the lawman now. He understood now why Sarah had been so hysterical.

Harding checked that his guns were fully loaded. Ritter and his cronies might have killed Jess and the sheriff. His job now was to ensure that they didn't kidnap Sarah.

He knew that they would try to encircle him and cut off any means of escape. He had witnessed too much to be allowed to get away. As he rounded another boulder, a stream of bullets whined their way towards him, most of them crashing harmlessly into the rocks next to him. He ducked, then loosed off a couple of shots of his own. He dropped to the dirt as more bullets whacked into the surrounding earth, then crawled cautiously on his belly, guns in hand, towards the direction of the shots, taking full advantage of the numerous boulders and rocks scattered on the range.

His eyes widened in surprise as he saw another man approaching him, bent double to gain cover from the rocks. 'Drop your guns,' Harding snarled.

The man stopped, his eyes staring at Harding. He licked his lips.

'Drop them.' Harding levelled his guns directly at the man's chest.

The man didn't obey. He raised both guns in Harding's direction.

Harding fired two shots in quick succession. The man's body crumpled, his eyes glazed with surprise as the shots thumped into him. An ugly gurgle rose from his throat, then he crashed to the ground, raising a cloud of dust as he landed.

Harding reloaded immediately. He jumped to his feet, expecting the dead man's friends to be heading his way having heard the sound of shots. But there was no sign of anybody. Then he heard Ritter's voice shouting at him.

'Harding. You'd better come on out into the open. Otherwise I'm gonna let my boys loose on this girl.' There was silence for a moment. 'You hear me, Harding?'

Harding kept quiet, hugging the rock behind which he was sheltering. He figured that even Ritter wouldn't harm the girl. No matter how hard and bloodthirsty he was, Ritter would know that his best card was to hold the girl and keep her well, so that he could use her as a bargaining chip until the time came for him to dispose of her. For there was no possibility of her being allowed to survive. Like Harding, she knew too much. Both of them were in the way of Jenkins' ambition, whatever that was, and he would do his best, through hired killers like Ritter, to silence them both.

'OK boys.' Harding heard Ritter's voice again, but this time it was lower, giving orders to his men. 'Go and flush him out. He's got to be silenced. And do a better job of it than you did this morning,' he snarled.

'Ain't you gonna help us?' one of them asked plaintively. 'I reckon he's plugged Menton already. And he shot up my arm this morning pretty bad.'

'Get to it, you lily-livered, yellow-bellied coyotes,' Ritter shouted. 'You've been well paid for the last two years. Now get out there and earn it.'

'You sure . . .'

'Don't argue,' snarled Ritter. 'Harding's a man, just like you and me and a bullet will stop him just as easily as any other man. Now get to it.'

'He can throw lead around better than us,' complained another voice. 'If we had a bunch of the boys with us, yeah, but on our own . . .'

'Harding knows what we've done here. He's got to be killed. Unless you want to be hanging from a rope within the week.'

Harding heard a string of curses coming from behind the rocks shielding one of the men. Then a voice shouted,

'What are you going to do? Just lie low and wait for us to do all the work?'

'I'm going back to the ranch with the girl,' snarled Ritter. 'I expect good news from you when you get back there. And so will Jenkins. Make sure you bury both bodies deep so that nobody will sniff them out.'

Harding stiffened at this news. He might get a chance to loose off a couple of shots at Ritter as he made to ride out. If Sarah was on another horse, trailing behind him, he'd be able to pick him off. That would discourage the others. They'd probably hightail it if Ritter was shot. He stood up and fired a hail of lead at the rocks that hid Ritter's cronies.

Then Harding heard the thunder of a horse galloping away. He cursed. Ritter was getting away. The sound of hooves faded into the distance. Knowing that Sarah was now out of danger of being blasted by his own bullets, at least for the time being, Harding resolved to flush out the remaining gunmen and deal with them.

He listened intently for any sound of movement. There was none. He crawled between the rocks, which gave him a certain amount of cover, and headed in the direction of the plaintive voices he had heard, minutes earlier, complaining to Ritter. He stopped and listened once again for any indication of movement. Breathing in deeply, he paused for a few seconds to regain his composure. Glancing around him, trying to determine his next move, he spotted three hand-sized pieces of rock. An idea immediately flashed into his head. He picked up the closest rock and hurled it twenty yards to his right. When it crashed into the dirt, there was a momentary pause, then a volley of bullets smashed into the boulders and dirt surrounding the spot where it had landed.

Harding glanced quickly to see where the lead was coming from then dashed between the rocks, circling behind the remaining gunmen. He padded forward until he could see their backs. They were talking quietly to each other.

'Drop your guns,' Harding ordered. Both his Colts were aimed directly at their backs. 'Don't try anything stupid. You won't even have time to half turn towards me.' His voice was harsh and cold.

The men froze. They tossed their guns into the dirt.

'Turn around. Real slow.'

The men turned to face him. Fear was etched into their faces. Perhaps Harding's reputation was known to them. Perhaps they were just yellow when they didn't have all the chips in their hands. 'Listen, feller,' the tall one said. 'We didn't kill the sheriff. It wasn't us. We just do as we're told.'

'Yeah, that's right,' his companion said. 'We're just a couple of cowpokes doin' what the boss tells us.'

'Like killing people and kidnapping women, huh?' said Harding sarcastically. 'Who killed my brother and Sheriff Turner?'

'Ritter,' the tall one said. 'We're not

professional killers like him. We just pack a gun like every other man in the West.'

Harding's eyes glittered with anger. He despised men like these. They were brave enough when they had the cover of a dozen men but on their own, their courage melted like snow in the sun. 'Move,' he snarled, indicating that they head for their horses. 'I'm taking you into town where you can tell the deputy sheriff what happened here.'

The taller man visibly shook. 'I . . . I had nothing to do with this,' he pleaded. 'Neither of us did. You take us into town and we'll tell the deputy whatever he wants to hear.'

'That's not what I want,' retorted Harding. 'I want the truth. Not your version of it.'

The tall man looked at his companion, who nodded. 'OK. We'll do anything you say. But it's Ritter you want. He's the killer.'

As they started walking slowly to their horses, the tall one turned around.

'Listen. Why don't we sort all this out now, before we get into town? If people see us in town word will get back to Jenkins and Ritter. Who knows what they'll do then?'

'Frightened, are you?' asked Harding. 'You've got every reason to be.'

The short, stubby man spoke for the first time. 'If we agree to talk, can you make sure that we'll be able to leave the territory? I don't like the idea of hanging around here once we've sold out to the law.'

Harding stared at them. He couldn't decide whether or not they were telling him the truth. But he wasn't taking any chances. 'I don't need your help to nail the men who killed my brother and the sheriff.' He pointed towards the prone body of Sheriff Turner. 'Strap his body on to his horse.'

'What about our guns? Can't we take them with us?' asked the tall man.

Harding smiled coldly. 'I'll take them. You won't be needing them for a while.'

A ball of red was setting slowly in the west when he herded the two men into town. Sheriff Turner's body hung limp on his horse, his arms swinging lazily to the motion of the horse's gait.

4

Harding headed straight for the sheriff's office. 'Get down,' he ordered curtly. 'Move.'

The two men obeyed him, grunting uneasily as they saw some townsfolk approaching to see what was happening. One of the first on the scene was Deputy Sheriff Colclough, who had just strolled out of the saloon.

'Who . . . who's that?' he asked, his eyes bulging wide. He looked more closely at the horse and the man slung over it. 'That's Ken Turner,' he exclaimed.

'That's right,' Harding said quietly. He dismounted, keeping a wary eye on his captives.

Colclough cleared his throat, momentarily unable to speak. 'By God, there'll be hell to pay for this. Did you . . . '

'No,' snapped Harding. 'I didn't. These two coyotes here had something to do with it, along with somebody else I'm sure you've heard of. Feller named Ritter.'

Colclough nodded. 'Yeah. I know Ritter,' he muttered. 'So did the sheriff. In fact, Ken didn't like him at all. He was always sniffing around Sarah when Ken wasn't about. Seems he fancied himself as a suitable beau.'

Colclough shook his head slowly. 'The sheriff got to hear about his pestering so he squared up to Ritter a couple of weeks ago.' Colclough paused and whistled slowly. 'We all thought there was going to be a showdown, but Ritter backed off at the last minute. Guess he's carried that grudge around with him ever since . . . and it looks as if he's finally settled the score.'

Harding's face tightened visibly. 'You mean that skunk's got designs on Sarah?'

'Yup,' Colclough replied.

'Get a posse together, right away.' A

note of panic had entered Harding's voice. 'Ritter's kidnapped Sarah. The sooner we go after him the sooner she'll be released.' He grimaced. 'If he harms that girl . . . '

At that moment, he felt a hand rest on his shoulder. Harding spun around and found himself looking into the steely, blue eyes of a grey-haired man aged around fifty. When he spoke, his voice was deep and gravelly. 'I'm Charles Jenson. Did you say that my daughter's been kidnapped?' Although his voice was low and deep, it was heavy with emotion.

'I'm afraid so,' responded Harding. 'The deputy sheriff is arranging for a posse to be organized, once he locks up these two,' he said. He looked at Colclough, who promptly nodded his head and shoved the two men Harding had captured towards the jailhouse.

Jenson turned to Harding. 'I own a fair amount of the land hereabouts, Mr . . . '

'Harding. Jim Harding.' He shook

Jenson's outstretched hand.

'As I was saying, Mr Harding, I own most of this town and the surrounding land. I'm also Mayor. Can I ask you to do me, and the town, a favour, seeing Colclough is going to be out with us chasing Ritter and trying to catch these killers?'

Harding eyed him. He didn't know what Jenson was going to ask him to do, but he figured that he was a man he could trust. Quite apart from that, if he did him a favour, one day he would be in a position to ask for the favour to be returned. 'Guess so,' he said.

Jenson motioned that he follow him into the sheriff's office. Inside, they watched Colclough lock up Ritter's side-kicks. 'I was just asking Harding here if he'll do us all a favour while we're out looking for Ritter.'

Colclough looked puzzled. 'What kind of favour?'

'The sheriff's dead. You're going to be out of town. Who's going to look after the place while you're gone?'

Colclough grunted. 'You have a point there.'

'Fetch me one of those deputy badges that the sheriff used to keep in the drawer,' said Jenson. 'I propose Harding as a deputy. I've heard some good things about him in the short time he's been here, even though I only met him just a couple of minutes ago. And he's got all the experience needed to make sure everything's OK while we're away on other business.' His face was etched in pain as he spoke. The news of his daughter's kidnapping must have shaken him to the core, but Harding could see that he still had the interests and welfare of the town, and the people in it, as one of his main concerns.

Colclough hauled open a drawer, pulled out a battered badge and flicked it across to Harding, who caught it deftly. 'I've worked with lawmen to bring some real bad hombres to book, but I've never had one of these before,' he said, weighing the small piece of metal in his hand. He pinned the badge to his shirt front.

They all walked outside. Colclough headed straight for the saloon and within a few minutes he had returned with a motley collection of men of all ages. Some of them appeared to be eager to hit the trail in pursuit of Ritter but others, mostly the older men, looked distinctly upset at having to leave their shots of booze and games of poker.

When they had all saddled up, amongst considerable noise and confusion, they set off in a cloud of dust, Colclough at their head. Harding watched them go, a strange, empty feeling churning in his gut. He had been left in total control of the town only days after arriving in the area. It was a situation he had not sought and, until he got used to it, he wasn't certain if he liked the idea.

He was about to go back into the sheriff's office to check on how the two hombres he had brought in were faring when he saw a flurry of dust on the outskirts of town. Somebody was returning.

Jenson's horse thundered to a halt beside Harding. He swung down from his horse and tied it to a hitching rail. He eyed Harding. 'That lot are on their way, but I don't think they're going to be very successful. As I rode out with them, I thought that a professional hunter, like you, might be the best bet I have of finding Sarah.' His eyes searched Harding's face for any sign of interest in what he was saying but Harding remained impassive. 'I'm a rich man, Harding. I'll make it worth your while to go after Ritter and his evil friends. If you bring my girl back, I'll make you a rich man.'

'I gave up man-hunting some time ago,' Harding replied. 'There was a reason for it and I'm not too anxious to start it all over again. You'd best leave it to the posse. I'm sure Colclough knows what he's doing. He knows the country around here and he must have plenty of experience of leading a posse.'

Jenson shook his head. 'Colclough's never led a posse in his life. He's been part of one but he's no leader of men. I think he's going to be lost out there,' he continued, jerking his head towards the open range. 'Go and track Ritter down. Get my daughter back for me, Harding.' His eyes stared wildly and flickered with fear.

Although the urge to avenge Jess's murder burnt within him, alongside his fierce desire to ensure Sarah's safety, he felt it best to let the law deal with the matter. 'I'm a stranger in these parts, Mr Jenson, so I'm at a real disadvantage compared to Colclough. He knows the terrain. What's more, he's the deputy sheriff. I can't take over the posse.'

'Sarah is my only child,' muttered Jenson. 'She's all my wife and I have. If Ritter hurts my Sarah, by God, I'll . . . '

'He won't hurt her,' interrupted Harding. 'He'd be crazy to do that. She's the best chance he has of getting out of the mess he's in. If he's got any sense, he'll use her as his way out of the county.'

A brief flash of relief lightened Jenson's features. As Harding studied his worn, weatherbeaten face, he wondered if Jenson really believed what he'd said. The truth of the matter was that neither he nor anybody else knew how Ritter would react. He appeared to be a totally unpredictable character with no qualms about killing. There was no reason to suppose he'd treat a woman any differently to a man. The only glimmer of hope was the fact that he seemed to have a soft spot for Sarah. But that was a two-edged sword. On the one hand, he might look after her more than he would an ordinary captive. On the other, he might view her capture as his only opportunity of ever possessing the woman he wanted. Harding grimaced and his fists tightened into two hard balls. 'He'd better not touch her,' he muttered quietly to himself. 'Else he'll have me to reckon with.'

'Did you say something?' Jenson asked.

Harding smiled grimly. 'The best thing for you to do is go home and comfort your wife. I'll bring you news the moment I hear any.'

Jenson shook his head sadly. 'I guess I'm too old to be riding with a posse. There's plenty of young fellers far more capable than me of finding that killer.'

'You'd only get in their way,' Harding agreed quietly. 'There's nothing worse for a posse than someone who's riding with grief in his heart and no concern for others. It might take some time to track Ritter down. The hunt for him will need men with stamina and clear heads.'

'Guess I don't have that at the moment. Couldn't even stay with them five minutes. When the notion came into my head that you'd do a better job than them I rode straight back here to talk to you. You're right. I'd be a hindrance.'

Harding walked Jenson to his home.

His wife, a well-built woman with slightly greying hair, greeted them and asked Harding if he'd care for some coffee. He declined, then added, 'Your husband has something to tell you, ma'am. Best if I leave you alone.' He turned to Jenson. 'The moment I hear anything . . . '

Jenson nodded.

'What is he talking about, dear?' Mrs Jenson's voice was suddenly strained and contained a hint of fear.

Harding turned away and headed back to the sheriff's office. He heard the front door of Jenson's house closing and wondered at the grief that household would suffer over the next few days. Maybe even over the next few weeks. And longer depending on how long it took to find and stop Ritter.

When he reached the sheriff's office it was dark. Only the pale yellow light thrown on to the street through the windows of the saloon lit his way.

As he stepped up on to the boardwalk to enter the sheriff's office, some hidden sense within him made him pause. He glanced around him quickly but all was quiet. He noted that the lamp which hung outside the door flooded the entrance to the office with light. Bad move to put that lamp there, he thought. Gives a clear view of anybody coming in or going out of the office. As that thought played on his mind, an icy shiver ran down his back as he realized that he was standing, momentarily, in the pool of light.

A tremendous crash rocked the night. A bullet thudded into the post only inches away from him. Another shot whined past his head and smashed through the window of the office. Harding threw himself to the floor and rolled out of the pool of light that had illuminated the whole of the boardwalk and made him such an easy target.

He winced and grunted with pain as his injured shoulder took the full effect of his fall. 'This is getting kinda crazy,' he muttered ironically. He had been very fortunate so far. But he had to put a stop to these attempts on his life. His luck couldn't hold out for ever.

Harding cursed under his breath. Was this an attempt to break the two hombres he had captured out of jail? If so, was it really possible that Ritter had returned to town knowing the danger he'd be in? What had Ritter done with Sarah if it was him? Perhaps it was somebody else. Maybe Jenkins. But why?

He didn't have time to think of anything else. Another hail of bullets crashed into the walls and boardwalk around him. He crawled along the bare wood on his belly and slid into an alley adjacent to the office. He pulled his Colt out of its holster and checked that it was fully loaded, then waited to see the flash of the guns directed at him.

He didn't have long to wait. The moment he had identified where the bushwhacker was situated, he loosed off a couple of shots of his own. He heard a cry of pain and then some groaning. Elated that his first shots had hit home, he cautiously crept out of the alley and was about to cross the road towards the sound of the groans when another shot whistled past him.

Harding retreated rapidly, throwing himself to the ground in the alley. At least two of them, he thought grimly. Who the hell are they? He reloaded his gun and waited for events to unfold. If they wanted him, they'd have to come and get him. That would give him a chance to pick them off because finding somebody who was well hidden in the pitch blackness of the alley was almost impossible.

Harding was playing a game of nerves with his assailants. He knew that the first person to crack, by making a rash move or exposing himself to try and flush the other out from under cover or to gain an advantageous position, would suffer the consequences. Harding was determined that it would not be him. He was under pressure from at least two gunmen, maybe more. He could ill afford to make a mistake. Well used to staking out his quarry in his years as a bounty hunter, he now had to draw on all that experience. It was a situation he had not thought he'd ever be in again when he first rode into this territory just a couple of days back. But now that he found himself lying in an alley, pinned down by bushwhackers' fire, he had no intention of succumbing without a fierce fight.

He lay quietly for several minutes. Nothing stirred. He knew that nobody would venture outdoors after the burst of gunfire because the only men left in town were too old or too frail to do anything about it. All the able-bodied men were in the posse. He wondered if this had been a deliberate ploy by Jenkins or Ritter, to empty the town of men and give them free rein to do what they wanted. If so, it was obvious what they were after. Either their cronies, who were, at that moment, languishing in jail. Or they're after me, he thought.

The creak of a foot on the boardwalk

made Harding stiffen. Somebody was approaching, very slowly. Harding lifted his Colt, aiming directly at the faint outline of the wall that lay to his right. Whoever was creeping down the boardwalk in front of the sheriff's office would have to cross in front of him to get to the other side of the alley. Unless the gunman was on his way to flush him out. In which case, there might be two of them, one coming at him from the front and one from the back.

Harding swiftly glanced to the back of the alley. It was enclosed by a large wall connecting both buildings on either side. He breathed easier. Nobody could attack him from the back. It had to be a frontal attack if there was going to be any move at all.

He waited, but nothing happened. He was beginning to get cold and his shoulder was aching like hell. Something had to be done. He could be trapped in the alley all night. Eventually, he might drop off to sleep and that would be when they'd get him. He began to have a certain degree of respect for his opponents. They weren't foolish. They were also playing a waiting game, secure in the knowledge that it would be at least sun-up before the posse returned.

Harding loosened one of his boots and slowly eased it off his foot. He grabbed it by the heel, listened for any sound of movement, then threw it across the alley towards the entrance. It thudded into the wooden wall. Simultaneously, the shadow of a man was illuminated in the weak light thrown by the lamp hanging outside the sheriff's office. He had stormed towards the alley at the sound of the noise and was pumping bullets into the wall at which Harding had thrown the boot.

Too anxious to finish the game, Harding thought as he took aim at the man's silhouette. He fired three shots in quick succession, feeling his Colt buck in his hand with a familiarity that reminded him of the trade he had only recently given up.

The man's body crumpled, He gave a loud screech which was transformed into a moaning groan as he lay slumped in the dirt. Harding waited. He was certain his shots had hit home but he had no intention of walking up to the gunman only to find that he was merely pretending to be hit and him pulling his gun and spraying bullets everywhere. Nor did he want to expose himself to the man's accomplice.

Minutes passed. The groans intensified, then subsided. Shortly afterwards, Harding heard a rattling noise coming from the man's throat. It became so distinct that the sound began to fill the alley. Only then was Harding convinced that the man had not been pretending. The sound he heard was the death rattle. This gunman had fired his last shot in anger. He was going to die in the dirt. In a cold alleyway. Alone.

Harding approached him cautiously. It was possible that the other gunman was waiting for him to show himself. But he doubted it. He'd probably taken off a long time ago. But Harding was in no hurry to join the unfortunate man whose body was now writhing in its death throes.

As he reached the dying man, Harding glanced quickly from side to side. There was nobody to be seen. Harding looked down at the body lying in front in him, unable to distinguish the man's features in the poor light. 'Soon find out who's behind all this,' he muttered to himself, feeling that he already knew the answer. What he couldn't figure out was why Jenkins, or Ritter, had come back to town when they must have known a posse would be out looking for them.

Harding hauled the body into the pool of light beneath the lamp. He laid it out and looked at the face. A shiver of shock rippled through him. He was looking at the dead features of Bret Carver.

5

Harding stared sadly at Carver's lifeless form. Several old men who had ventured outside shuffled cautiously towards him. They looked at him nervously. The oldest cleared his throat and spat a stream of black tobacco juice into the dirt. 'What's been goin' on here, young fella?'

Harding turned to face him. 'A grudge that took a long time dying has been laid to rest,' he said quietly, feeling some remorse at the killing. Then he shrugged his shoulders and dismissed such thoughts. Carver knew what he was getting into when he tried to gun him down. Harding couldn't be sure of the exact reasons, but recalled his own thoughts about blood being thicker than water. Maybe that was what all this was about. Carver simply couldn't bear the thought of the man who had killed his father and brother being around him.

Harding glanced at the men who surrounded him. 'Come on. Pick him up and take him to the feller who plants them in the ground in these parts.'

The men grunted and began to haul Carver's limp body out of the alleyway. Suddenly, remembering the other man he had shot, Harding ran across the road and into the shadows where he had tried to pick off Carver's companion. He walked slowly, Colt in hand. He doubted if the man was still there, having witnessed what had happened to Carver, but he was taking no chances.

He felt his way along the side of the wall. A cold wind whistled down between the buildings, making him shiver. Four yards into the alley, he stumbled against something solid lying in the dirt. He knelt down and felt the cold, clammy skin of a dead man. Harding gave a low whistle. He'd got them both.

He grabbed the man by the legs and

began to pull him into the dim light so that he could have a look at his face. His identity might indicate why Carver had tried to plug him. If this feller he was hauling was an old gunhand who had ridden with Carver's father and brother, maybe this was a case of revenge. If not, perhaps something else was behind the ambush.

The man's face revealed nothing to Harding. It was a face he had never seen before. He certainly hadn't ridden with old man Carver. Before he had any more time to ponder on why Carver had tried to plug him, a rapid series of shots shattered the peace of the night and reverberated throughout the town. Harding dropped the man's legs and hurried towards the sound of the gunfire, painfully aware that he was now responsible for the well-being of the town and its inhabitants until the posse returned.

A crowd had gathered outside a rather undistinguished building barely a dozen yards down the street from the sheriff's office. A fierce fire was raging inside and Harding could already see the flames licking the wooden front of the building. He ran towards it and was quickly joined by others as they flooded out of houses and the saloon.

'There must be somebody in there,' said a grizzly old man who was tottering on unstable legs and gesticulating wildly as Harding pushed past him. 'I heard some people arguing in there as I was passing. Then I heard some shots.'

'Who owns that place?' Harding demanded.

'It's Jenson's office. That's where he carries on all his law work. He's an attorney.'

'What the hell would anybody want to start a fire in a law office for?' enquired Harding incredulously to nobody in particular.

''Cause, young feller, there's a lot of money stashed away in his safe.'

'How do you know that?' Harding asked.

'The payroll for his whole workforce was delivered from the bank this afternoon,' replied the old man. 'Everyone in town knows that. Told Jenson many a time he was taking a risk having all that money in his office rather than keeping it safe in the bank until he was ready to pay it out to his workers.'

'Get some water!' Harding shouted. 'I'm going to try and see if anybody is alive in there.'

Several of the men scrambled to get pails. Harding waited until they had filled them with water and were standing in front of the blazing building, waiting for his command. 'When I shout, throw all the water you have over the entrance then go get some more and do the same thing again. It might cool things down just long enough for me to get in there and see what's happened.'

The first shower of water drenched the blazing entrance and extinguished enough flames to allow Harding to dash through the door, his red bandanna covering his mouth to prevent the acrid fumes from choking him. He stumbled into the room, crashing into a desk which he failed to see in the darkness. Dense smoke was billowing out from a back room. Harding kicked wide the half open door leading to the room but was beaten back by a wall of flame that suddenly jumped at him the moment the door was forced open. 'Over here,' he shouted. 'More water over here!'

Three men hurried towards where he was standing and doused some of the raging flames. They hurried off, their places immediately taken by more men who heaved heavy pailfuls of water on to the fire. After ten minutes, they had doused the flames sufficiently for Harding to rush into the room to see if anybody had been trapped inside. He knew that if they had, they'd be dead by now. If the shots he'd heard hadn't killed them, the smoke and intense heat certainly would.

He shielded his face from the blistering heat that still hung in the air.

He saw the badly burnt body of a man sprawled on the floor, close to the door, a leather bag grasped in his hand. Harding pulled the body out of the back room and into the street. He turned the man over. Despite the severe burns that the fire had inflicted on him, the face was clearly that of Charles Jenson.

But it wasn't the fire or the smoke that had killed him. Harding immediately noticed the large red stain that covered the partially charred remnants of the shirt he was wearing. At least two bullets had been pumped into his chest from close range. Probably the very shots Harding had heard whilst trying to identify the man he himself had plugged.

Prising the leather bag from Jenson's hand, which was still hot from the flames that had almost devoured it, he opened it wide and peered inside. The charred remains of a few bank notes was all the bag contained.

'Somebody was after the payroll

. . . or the money he kept for some of his clients.' The grizzly old man he had spoken to earlier sucked on his yellowing teeth. 'That feller sure was taking a risk keeping all that money in his own safe.'

'That kind of money should have been left in the bank,' Harding agreed.

'He didn't trust banks,' the old man continued, scratching at the thick, grey stubble on his chin. 'Especially the one in this town. It's been hit twice in the last year. Some folks think it's the same bunch who've been doin' the rustling but nobody's caught any of them so nobody really knows for sure.'

'Hey!' The shout was loud and excited. 'There's a trail of blood leading to the back door. Must have been hurt pretty bad even if he did escape.'

Harding ran into the office again. He saw the blood splashed on the floor in the middle of the room. Close by was a gun. Must be Jenson's, he thought. At least he managed to plug whoever killed him.

Grabbing a still burning stick of wood to light the way, he followed the trail of blood out into the back alley. Gradually, the trail petered out. The man must have attempted to staunch the wound, knowing that he was leaving a trail. He must also have known that if he carried on losing blood to that extent he'd soon be a goner.

'He's hightailed it out of town by now,' muttered Harding to the old man who had followed him. 'Whoever he is.'

'Guess you're right.'

Harding walked slowly back to the sheriff's office. The excitement of the last hour or so had occupied him so much that his attention had been diverted from the situation Sarah Jenson was in. Now, if she survived her brutal confinement with the dangerous criminal who had killed his brother, on her release she would have to cope with the added shock of learning that her father had been murdered. These thoughts reminded Harding that Jenson's wife needed to be told what had happened. He walked back to find the old man.

'What's your name, oldtimer?'

'Coleman.'

'Can you come with me to Jenson's house? I've got to break the news to his widow and find out if anybody came to see her husband tonight.'

As Harding walked alongside Coleman, his thoughts turned again to the dilemma Sarah was in and whether the posse had found Ritter. He worried whether the deputy sheriff was up to the task he had been landed with. Ritter was a killer. It would take someone with a great deal of experience to track him down. Someone as cunning as himself. Harding began to regret not having gone with them. He wondered whether he had avoided his duty by taking what seemed to be the easy option of staying to protect the town until the posse returned, rather than being out there hunting for a dangerous killer.

Not that he considered telling a woman that her husband had been murdered was an easy option. And the events of the last couple of hours had been far more hectic than he had bargained for.

'I'm afraid I have some bad news, Mrs Jenson.' Harding saw an anguished look flash across her face but she regained her composure very quickly.

'Come . . . come in,' she said hesitantly.

Both Harding and the old man followed her into the house, which was furnished in a very comfortable and homely manner. A woman whose home life is very important to her, thought Harding, knowing how devastating the news he had to break to her would be. He had done it before, to the widows of men he had tracked down and killed. The terrible looks of anguish and despair he had seen on those women's faces was one of the reasons he had decided to hang up his guns. Although, ironically, he was now using his guns more often than he had for quite some time.

'I'm afraid,' Harding started uncomfortably, and in as sympathetic a voice as he could, 'that your husband has been killed.'

The woman gasped and clutched at her throat. Tears began to form in her eyes but she brushed them away and cleared her throat. 'When I heard the knock at the door after the explosion and all that shooting,' she said quietly, 'I knew that something was badly amiss.'

'I know it's a very difficult time for you, Mrs Jenson,' Harding continued quietly, 'but I really need to know if you have any idea who your husband was meeting tonight.'

She shook her head. 'I was doing some sewing in the front room when I heard Charles talking to someone at the door. I assumed it was business as Charles didn't invite him in so I stayed where I was.' Her eyes filled with tears once again and this time she sobbed gently and dabbed her eyes with a lace handkerchief. 'That was the last time I heard him talking. If only I had known . . . ' Her voice trailed away.

'Did you recognize the other man's voice?' Harding pressed gently.

She shook her head. 'I really didn't take much notice of what was being said,' she replied. 'But I did get the impression that the other man was a bit hoarse. His voice seemed a bit strained.'

'Thank you.' Harding looked at her, compassion flooding through him at the sight of the newly bereaved woman. 'Would you like me to call the doctor?'

She shook her head. 'I'd like to be on my own.'

The old man, who had remained silent throughout, patted her gently on the back. 'I'll call in the morning to see how you are.'

Coleman went home. Harding, after having ordered Carver's body and that of his compatriot to be taken to the gravedigger, decided to return to the sheriff's office to bunk down for the night. There was nothing he could do about tracking Jenson's killer until the morning. Although he had plenty of experience of running down badmen there was no point in starting till sun-up.

As he slumped into his chair, wondering once again what progress the posse had made in tracking Ritter, there was a shout outside his window. Seconds later, a fist pummelled his door. 'Come in,' he shouted.

A dishevelled-looking man, his shirt-tail flapping behind his back and his hair matted down with grease, rushed in and started gesticulating wildly. 'Found a hoss tied to a hitchin' post just down the road. Reckon it belonged to the man who plugged Jenson. You know why I think that? Cause that hoss belongs to Ritter, the killer who hangs out at the Jenkins place.' His words tumbled out in a breathless flurry.

Harding shot out of the chair he had been sprawling in. 'You sure about that?' he asked.

'Course I'm sure. I feed the damn thing every time Ritter comes into town. I work at the livery and I ain't ever seen Ritter's hoss tied up and just left like that.'

'Why did he leave his horse behind if he was loaded down with cash taken from Jenson's safe?' Harding was puzzled. 'Seems to me that's exactly when he'd need his horse, to make a quick getaway . . . unless . . . he was so badly wounded he just grabbed the first horse he could and crawled into the nearest hole he could find to get his wounds seen to.'

'In that case, you'd better head straight for Jenny Logan's. He's been seen hanging around there with a gal named Lizzie Morgan.'

Harding smiled. 'I take it that's the local cathouse.'

'Sure is. Two miles outside town 'cause the good ladies of Sentenas wouldn't allow such a place inside the town boundary.'

'Thanks.' A couple of minutes later, Harding was on his buckskin heading straight for Logan's. Apart from trying to figure out how Ritter could have returned to town so quickly when he had Sarah as a captive, Harding was also puzzled how Ritter, a known killer, had persuaded Jenson to take him to his office. He must have threatened him. But why? Why would he have risked everything to come back to town just to raid Jenson's safe? Harding was still chewing on these thoughts when he saw the red lamps dangling outside Jenny Logan's.

6

Harding approached Jenny Logan's with caution. If Ritter was inside, there was no guarantee he was enjoying himself with Lizzie Morgan. More likely, he was suffering from the flesh wound that had made him seek shelter there in the first place. And a man like Ritter would be like a wounded animal. Afraid, alert and dangerous.

Harding heard the raucous shouting of the men and the shrill laughter of the girls in the cathouse long before he could clearly see the building. The flickering light that filtered through the red net curtains lit his way towards the house, which lay outside the town limits on the edge of the prairie. It was located there for a purpose. If a man was visiting, he was there for one reason and one reason only. Except Ritter, maybe. If he was in cahoots with Lizzie

Morgan, she might be willing to help him. Especially if he let her feast her eyes on the money taken from Jenson.

The boards at the side of the house creaked gently as Harding eased himself on to them to try and get a better view of who was inside and to check if he was in any danger of being seen. He edged his way slowly to the side door, his heart pounding and his palms beginning to moisten in a way that brought back vivid memories of earlier duels and stake outs.

He raised his hand to wipe away a trickle of sweat that had begun to run down the side of his forehead when a thunderous explosion inside his head blackened his vision. He crashed to his knees, then felt a vicious kick to his ribs. He coughed, then attempted to turn around to see who or what had assaulted him.

A flash of pain blurred his senses and he felt the salty taste of blood in his mouth. He coughed again. Another blow hit him in the head. As he stumbled to his feet, a crashing fist felled him again. The taste of blood now filled his mouth. He spat out the salty spittle, feeling the cut on the side of his tongue. But he had no time to consider such matters. He heard a harsh laugh from a man standing to his right. At the sound of the man's cruel, taunting laughter, anger burst inside Harding. For a moment, it completely displaced the pain coursing through his body.

He lunged at the shape of the man on his right, grappling him at waist level. With a resounding crash, they fell through the door and hit the wooden floor together, causing it to shake. Another flood of pain burst through Harding's body. He grabbed the man around his neck and began to squeeze. He heard a choking noise and gurgling sounds as the man attempted to free himself.

Just when Harding thought he was beginning to still the fight in his unknown assailant, a vicious kick to his groin made him convulse and scream in agony. He released the man's throat and clutched his groin. The excruciating pain that coursed through him made him double up.

After only a few seconds, another kick to the head stunned him. He shook his head and tried to focus on the man who towered above him. A vicious smile, revealing stained, yellowed teeth, split Ritter's face as he looked down at Harding, spreadeagled on the floor.

The fury that Harding felt at that moment released a surge of energy within him. He leapt to his feet and swung at Ritter's surprised face. The sound of his fist crunching into his opponent's jaw gave Harding a degree of elation that he had not felt for a very long time. He saw Ritter's knees buckle beneath him at the strength of the blow. Taking his chance, Harding unleashed another punch at Ritter's face. This time, Ritter took evasive action. His head swayed to one side, avoiding Harding's clenched fist.

As soon as the punch slipped past him, Ritter kicked again at Harding's groin. But this time Harding was ready for him. He grabbed Ritter's foot, lifted it up high, then threw him on to his back. Ritter sprawled on the floor, his hands clawing at fresh air as he fell. Harding took a few quick steps towards him, then aimed a kick at his adversary's head. A spray of crimson blood burst out of Ritter's nose the moment the kick made contact, followed by a terrible scream as the agony of the blow seared through the man's system.

Harding's hand slid down to the Colt .45 in his holster. Before he had time to draw it, another thunderous blow to the back of his head sent him reeling. As he crashed to the floor, he managed to twist around to see who had attacked him. To his surprise, he saw a slight woman holding a gun in her right hand, her left hand covering her mouth in a gesture which, to Harding, signified guilt. Then a fog of unconsciousness swamped him.

'No . . . not here . . . please.' Harding heard the words faintly. He opened his eyes to find himself staring into the cold barrel of a Colt .45 held in Ritter's hand. The woman was standing beside him, holding his arm and trying to restrain him from blasting Harding's head off. 'If you kill him here Mr Kitson will get into an awful lot of trouble and so will all the girls.'

Harding managed a wry smile as the haze of pain began to clear. Even though she was less concerned about him than the reputation of the cathouse and its occupants, at least she was giving him some time to recover his senses and, maybe, a chance to survive.

A loud knocking on the door distracted Ritter's wavering attention. He walked unsteadily across to the door and opened it. Still lying on the floor, Harding could just see the man who stood framed in the doorway. He was a small, fat man dressed in a bright red waistcoat and black trousers with grey stripes. 'What the hell's goin' on here?' he asked. 'I run a clean house. I don't want no trouble, you hear?' His eyes swivelled past Ritter and searched the room. They alighted momentarily on the girl and then on the figure of Harding, who by this time had managed to struggle on to his elbows.

'What's he doin' down there?' the man spluttered. 'I don't want no trouble here. Get him outa here.'

Ritter's face twisted into a vicious snarl. He took a step towards Kitson, his fists beginning to clench into hard balls of iron. A sudden scream from the girl distracted him. 'No. Don't.' Her hands flew to her face in some sort of primitive defence mechanism.

Ritter stopped, then turned to look at Harding. Through the haze of pain, Harding saw the cruel, vicious smile on his hard, weatherbeaten face. 'I've taken you once, mister,' Ritter snarled. 'And you're damn lucky I don't finish you off right now. If you cross my path again, I'll plant you in the ground.'

Then he was gone, shoving Kitson out of the way and leaving a tearful girl behind him. Harding grunted, pain surging through him again. It had been a long time since he had felt this sore and it only brought to mind his thoughts of a few days earlier. He was too old and slow for this type of work. But what else could he do but stand and fight when his very existence was threatened? Turn tail and run? That was no answer. He would have to stand his ground. He struggled slowly to his feet, helped by the pale trembling arm of the girl he took to be Lizzie Morgan.

'Thanks,' he grunted, as he retrieved his hat from the floor. He heard the thunder of horses' hooves fading into the distance and knew that his man was lost to him that evening.

'I'm sorry about . . . ' Lizzie Morgan began, her eyes darting from side to side as if looking for a place to escape. A muscle began twitching nervously in the side of her cheek. 'If I hadn't hit you he'd have killed me . . . '

'It's OK,' Harding assured her. He wiped his brow and replaced the hat on his head. 'I don't hold you responsible, I have a fair idea what he'd have done to you if you'd gone against him.'

The girl gave a thin smile. 'Thanks.'

Harding made his way down to his horse which he had tethered at the back of the cathouse. 'Goddammit,' he exclaimed. A feeling of fury and frustration burst inside him when he saw that Ritter had released his horse. He'd have to walk back to town.

Two hours later, his mouth and throat dry and his head thundering from a pounding headache, Harding slumped into the chair in the sheriff's office. 'Didn't make a very good job of your first night on duty,' he murmured to himself. 'Maybe you should just hand this badge in . . . ' But even as he spoke, he knew he couldn't turn his back on the commitment he had made. If he did, he'd be known as a coward wherever he went. That was one thing nobody had ever dared call Jim

Harding to his face and they weren't about to start now.

He brewed himself some strong black coffee and took a sip. He sat down, stuck his feet up on the desk and slowly relaxed into the comfort of the old, worn, leather chair. His eyelids began to droop as a wave of tiredness and lethargy swept over him. He placed the mug of coffee on the desk and tilted his hat forward over his forehead to cover his eyes. Within minutes, the long fingers of exhaustion had carried him into a deep sleep.

A loud thudding stirred Harding. Instinctively, his body reacted but then his weary brain reassured him that nothing was amiss and he drifted back to the deep slumber from which he had been stirred. Then two sharp cracks on the solid wooden door of the sheriff's office made him sit up like a scared jack rabbit. Somebody was out there after all. He grabbed his Winchester and checked that his Colt was filled with five slugs. Cautiously, he walked to the door and opened it.

A man stood on the boardwalk, his stetson pulled low over his forehead to shield his eyes. The faint glow flickering from the lamp hanging outside the office was insufficient to light the man's features.

'Remember me, Harding?' The voice was cold and menacing.

'Nope.'

'Sure you do.' As he spoke, the man pushed the front of his stetson back slightly to allow some light to fall on his face. It was hard and cruel, with a deep, white scar running down the right cheek. His eyes were black and cold. 'You stole $10,000 from me seven years ago.'

Harding groaned. As if he didn't have enough trouble with Ritter and the rest of them, here was some idiot he had never met saying he had swindled him. But the man's voice stirred vague memories in the deep recesses of his mind. Although the faint light from the lamp had only allowed him the briefest glimpse of the man's face, somewhere he had heard that voice before.

'The San Remo stake out,' the stranger said.

'Bob Tournier,' breathed Harding. His memory flashed back to the young man he had faced down whilst both of them had been after the same hombres who had robbed the First State Bank of San Remo. They had both been tracking those hard-hearted killers for many months, as had many other bounty hunters, but only the two of them had persevered.

One, a fresh-faced youngster with more balls than brains, and Harding, the hardened professional who had stared into more killers' eyes than the youngster had bullets in his gun belt. Tournier had backed down then, but Harding could tell from the man's tone that he had no intention of repeating the mistakes of his youth. Tournier was now a hardened professional himself and it was obvious that he was in no mood to compromise.

'That was all a very long time ago,' Harding muttered, his hand slipping down to the Colt strapped against his right thigh.

'Sure is,' mused Tournier. 'Never thought I'd cross paths with you again. But strange things sure do happen in life. When someone goes to the trouble of telegraphing me, saying he wants somebody taken care of . . . somebody by the name of Jim Harding . . . well, naturally, I thought back to the good old days.'

'Who was that?'

'Feller by the name of Carver.'

Harding nodded.

'Only trouble is, the darned fool tried to do the job himself before I got here. So when I arrived, I found out I didn't have a job.'

'So what are you aiming to do now?'

'Guess I'm just naturally lucky.' Tournier's face split into a deceptively warm smile but his eyes remained cold as ice. 'Having nothing to do, seeing as how this fool had got himself shot up by you, I went to the local cathouse to enjoy the fruits of the ladies that grace that wonderful establishment. Well, I got talking briefly with this feller who showed up in a hurry with blood dripping from him. Seems you upset him as well.' He paused and laughed. 'You sure as hell don't seem to be making many friends in these parts. So I have a job to do after all . . . protecting Ritter's back. And I get a bonus if I help him plant you in the ground. He's real upset with you.'

'I faced you down once before, Tournier, because you knew that I was faster and tougher than you, and I'll do it again if I have to.'

Tournier's grin faded. 'You're dealing with more than a fresh-faced kid now, Harding.'

'Maybe so. But you'll end up the same way as Carver if you take me on.'

'Pity that I'm only here to deliver a message this evening,' Tournier said with feigned regret. 'The showdown'll have to wait.' Tournier turned his back and stepped off the boardwalk to his horse. 'Giddup boy.' He gently coaxed the animal up on to the boardwalk and brought him to a halt outside the sheriff's office, directly in front of Harding. He took out a knife and slashed the ropes that bound some kind of bundle on the horse's back. It fell to the boards with a hollow thud. Before it had time to come to rest, Tournier had turned it with his foot. The lifeless body that lay prostrate on the boardwalk had its chest hacked open by at least three shots and the eyes, still open, stared lifelessly at the stars above. A macabre expression of surprise and fear was frozen on the cold face.

'Feller by the name of Jenkins who tried to double-cross Ritter. That was the result,' Tournier muttered.

7

Harding stared down at Jenkins' mutilated body. For the first time, icy fingers of fear began to claw at him. The men he was facing were ruthless killers, fast as rattlesnakes and ten times more deadly. Was he really fast enough to handle them? He'd soon find out.

Tournier left without another word, giving Harding a scornful, dismissive glance as he mounted his horse. It was as if he knew the former bounty hunter's time had come and gone. The balance of power had shifted in his favour and he had every intention of letting Harding know it. He thundered down the boardwalk, the iron-clad hooves of his horse crashing along the wooden boards. The animal flew off the end, Tournier giving a long, loud whoop of elation as horse and rider sailed through the air. Within seconds, they had disappeared, leaving behind only a small cloud of dust.

An hour had passed by the time Harding found the gravedigger and handed him Jenkins' body for safe keeping until burial the next day.

'Wakin' me up at this time of night,' the gravedigger complained plaintively. 'Why don't folks get themselves killed at a godly hour?' He looked at Harding with a sour expression on his face. 'Planning on killing the whole town? This makes five already.'

Harding shook his head in disbelief as the old man, his broken teeth stained black with tobacco smoke, carried on muttering and complaining about being hauled from his bed to do his job. As he slowly walked back to the sheriff's office, exhaustion seeping back into his bones, he began to consider the unenviable situation in which he found himself. It had only been a couple of days since he had arrived at a place where he thought he was going to make a new start, away from all the bloodshed of his recent past.

The shock of finding Jess and the pain of knowing that the woman he wanted was in the hands of a man who would show her no mercy burnt away like a smouldering torch inside him. A man who wanted him dead and who had improved his chances of getting what he wanted by employing a bounty hunter whose only code of conduct was governed by how much money he could make out of a kill. A man who cared for nothing but himself.

Harding shook his head slowly. He had to think this through and find a way of getting out of this mess. But first he had to get some sleep.

He slumped into one of the bunks at the back of the sheriff's office, normally used to house the town drunks until they sobered up for release the following morning. But he was fated not to get much sleep. The thunder of hooves woke him up with a start. The posse had returned.

The deputy sheriff spoke first.

'Nothing. Absolutely nothing.' He took off his hat and wiped the sweat from his face with his hand. 'When we got to the Jenkins place, the shack was all burnt out. There was no sign of Jenkins, Ritter or the girl. I don't know what happened out there but it sure doesn't look good for Sarah Jenson.'

A sudden high-pitched scream split the early morning air. The distraught figure of Sarah's mother, who had hurried out of the house the moment she had heard the posse returning, screamed again, then started sobbing. She had obviously heard the deputy's views on Sarah's plight.

'Take her back to the house,' Harding said to one of the cowpokes. 'She's not doing herself any good by listening to what happened back there. Tell her that if we find Sarah or hear anything, she'll be the first to be told.'

As the cowpoke led the forlorn figure of Mrs Jenson back home, Harding turned to the posse. 'The reason you didn't find Jenkins is because he was delivered to me a few hours ago.' He nodded towards the boardwalk. 'He was dumped there by an old compatriot of mine, a killer by the name of Tournier.'

There was an audible gasp from some of the posse when Tournier's name was mentioned. 'I see some of you have heard about him. Well, he delivered Jenkins' body to me with the message that Ritter had killed him and that I was going to be next. He was very polite about it. But he was also deadly serious. And the reason I know is because Ritter is paying him to do the killing. The first real chance he gets.'

Harding eyed the posse. Several of them shuffled uncomfortably in their saddles. Others avoided his gaze. 'What I need to know is how many of you folks are going to ride with me, today, to track these killers down and bring them to justice.'

A hush fell over the assembled body of men. Nobody stirred. 'Ritter killed your sheriff,' Harding shouted. 'I also believe he killed your mayor.'

The news of the mayor's death was met, initially, with a deathly hush. Then, frightened anxious faces peered at each other and the silence was broken by low mutterings. Harding managed to catch what one man was saying: 'If he's killed the mayor and the sheriff, he could kill anyone in town who makes a stand against him.'

Harding could hardly believe what he was hearing. 'Are you just going to let him get away with it?' he demanded. 'Are you going to leave a young, defenceless woman in his hands to do with as he pleases?'

'What you've got to realize,' began the deputy sheriff, 'is that these folks have families of their own. They don't want to get into a war with bounty hunters and professional killers. What would happen if these fellers called in some more of their friends to help them out?' There was a general but muted chorus of agreement to these sentiments from the posse.

'Colclough's right.' The speaker was

a well-built man with a florid face. 'Why should we risk everything for a couple of dead men and a girl who's probably dead already? If you have a quarrel with these killers, Harding, it's up to you to sort it out.'

The flames of anger and contempt Harding had begun to feel for these men were fanned into a raging fire. 'What kind of men do you call yourselves?' he yelled at them. 'Your sheriff and mayor have been murdered, one of your community has been kidnapped and all you can think about are your own skins. Don't you people realize that the woman Ritter kidnapped could just as easily have been your daughter? Don't you know that if you let him get away with this he'll be back and one of you might be next?'

Harding threw his deputy's badge into the dirt. 'If you people don't want to help yourselves, you're not worth wearing a badge for.' He strode towards his horse, swung into the saddle and rode out of town, heading back to the patch of land he had thought would bring him peace and tranquillity. Instead, he thought ruefully, it's given me the biggest headache I've ever had.

When he'd been a bounty hunter, he'd known what to expect. The taste of danger and death had been in his mouth and formed part of his life for so long that he had grown used to it. 'But,' he reasoned, 'when a man leaves that kind of life behind him, gets a scrap of land he hopes to cultivate, maybe raise a herd of beef, he expects life to be more peaceful, more civilized.' As he rode towards his ranch, he continued his reflections on how often life threw up dirt in a man's face just when he thought he could relax and enjoy it.

His ranch was lush and green. All the land spread out before him, as far as the eye could see, was his. Then, he lowered his head in sadness, knowing that Jess would never share it with him. He had vowed to find his killers. And he would, knowing now who they were. Even without the help of any of the townsfolk. This was something he couldn't run away from. And when he had finished that business, there was always Sarah. Maybe he would have her to share his life with.

Harding took a real pride in riding across his land. The shack that passed as his ranch house came into view. It stood, solid and welcoming, nestling beneath the high rocks at its back.

He tied up his horse, walked up to the front door and paused. He breathed a heavy sigh of regret, wondering when the peace that clothed his land at that very moment would be reflected in his own life.

He pushed the door open and stepped inside. Almost immediately, he felt there was something wrong.

His eyes took only a second to adapt to the gloom. Then he saw Sarah Jenson. Her eyes were red rimmed and tears were streaming down her cheeks. A sudden feeling of panic gripped him. Time seemed to stand still as he tried to figure out what on earth she was doing there. Then he felt the cold steel pressing into the back of his neck and a rough, rasping voice grated into his ear. 'Hello, sucker.'

Harding froze. His heart pounded vigorously in his chest and his mouth had suddenly become very dry. He tried to moisten his lips but failed.

'Drop your gun belt, real slow.'

Harding did as he was told. The belt slid off him and dropped to the floor with a thud.

'Turn around.'

Harding tore his eyes away from the tear-streaked face of Sarah Jenson and turned to face the man who held the gun against his head.

'Welcome.' Ritter's face was creased in a hard, cruel smile. 'How does it feel to have only five minutes left to live?'

Harding could see Ritter searching his face for the slightest sign of fear. Harding resolved not to give him any indication of the turmoil he was feeling inside. If he was going to die, he'd go with dignity. He'd be damned if he'd give this scum the satisfaction of seeing him suffer or beg for mercy. But he had no intention of dying. Not just yet. He had a woman to protect. Maybe a woman who would one day share his life if he took good care of her. He stared, without a flicker, straight into Ritter's eyes. 'Go ahead. Pull the trigger,' he said.

The smile vanished from Ritter's face. He was not expecting this type of behaviour from a man who had the barrel of a gun pressed against his temple. Momentarily, he seemed disorientated. His lips parted as if to speak. Harding saw his chance and took it.

His head jerked to one side, out of the direct line of the gun and, at the same time, his right fist came up and crashed straight into Ritter's jaw. The blow sent Ritter careering backwards. He sprawled against the side of the house with both arms flung wide, his legs crumpling beneath him at the force of the blow.

Harding leapt on him, tearing the

gun out of his hand. A wave of intense relief washed over Harding as he felt the gun nestling in his palm. It felt good to have the upper hand. 'On your feet,' he snapped. 'You and I are going to have a chat with the deputy sheriff about murder and kidnapping.' He emptied the chambers of Ritter's gun, the bullets tumbling and dancing on the wooden floor of the shack. Harding threw the gun across the room. 'You won't be needing that where you're going. Now get on your feet. You have an appointment to keep.'

Harding could hardly believe that he saw a grin spreading across Ritter's face. For a moment, he thought it must be a show of bravado which some trapped men used to try and intimidate their captors. But even Ritter's eyes, the mirror of the soul, which gave away a man's true feelings, gazed back at him calmly and defiantly. The preposterous thought that the girl was going to double-cross him and take Ritter's side was dismissed as soon as he thought of it. He glanced quickly across at her. She stood, shivering with fear and terror, in the corner of the room.

'You're the one with the appointment, Harding. With death.'

Harding stiffened. Fingers of fear began crawling up and down his spine. He had heard that rasping voice only hours earlier. He swore at himself. How could he have been so stupid as to let himself make two mistakes in such a short period of time? He had been so careful, so meticulous as a bounty hunter, weighing up all the odds against a successful capture and considering all the hunted man's options. Now, he was blundering about like an amateur.

Ritter's grin widened. 'Meet my new partner. He was hiding out back. Just in case he was needed.'

'Drop that gun, Harding,' said Tournier menacingly. 'Or the girl gets her head blown off first . . . then you.'

Harding threw down his gun.

'Now turn around so's I can get a proper look at you. It's been a long time since you stole that money off me.'

Harding figured that as long as he played along with them, the longer he'd live and the more chance he'd have for an opening to take them.

'You've grown older. And more careless.' Tournier tipped back his hat with the barrel of his gun as he spoke. 'Ritter tells me you're some kind of rancher now.'

Harding nodded. 'That's right.'

'You should have stuck to bounty hunting. You get respect from folk if you do that. It's a respect born out of fear. Nobody respects a rancher, clawing away in the dirt trying to make a few dollars for himself. It's no life for a man.'

'You reckon.'

Tournier's lips curled in disdain. 'I don't reckon. I know.'

'How come?'

Tournier's face flushed slightly. 'My folks were ranchers. And they were poor. What did ranching do for them? Nothing. A bunch of redskins raided the place, killed my father and then raped my mother and sister. They left them all dead . . . '

'If you're finished talking about your family history,' interrupted Ritter sarcastically, 'perhaps you could throw me that gun of yours so that I can get rid of him once and for all.'

Tournier turned his head sharply towards Ritter, contempt etched on his face. 'What about the money you promised me? This seems as good a time as any to get it, seeing as I've just helped you out.'

'You'll get your money,' Ritter snarled. 'Just throw me that gun of yours so I can finish him off and get the hell out of here.' Ritter paused, waiting for Tournier to obey him. The other man made no move. 'I hired you to help me get rid of this hombre. You'll get the money when the job's done and not before. Then you can go your own way.'

Tournier shook his head slowly. 'I don't trust you, Ritter.'

The expression on Ritter's face changed immediately. He realized that he was not going to get what he wanted from Tournier by duress. A wily look crept into his eyes and he laughed in an attempt to ease the tension. 'What the hell are you talking about? Your business is almost done here and soon you're going to walk away with over two hundred dollars.'

'I don't think so,' Tournier replied. His coal-black eyes glinted greedily and narrowed as he continued to stare at Ritter. 'I reckon there's more owing to me than that.'

Ritter suddenly scrambled to his feet, his eyes wide and staring. 'What's that noise?' he exclaimed.

Harding looked quickly from one man to the other. A sudden flash of uneasiness flew across both their faces. He too could just hear the cause of their concern — the faint rumble of horses' hooves in the distance. And there was only one place they could be heading. Not only was there no other house around for miles, the sound of the pounding hooves grew louder as every second passed.

'Come on. Give me that gun of yours so I can finish him off,' snapped Ritter.

'I don't think so.' Tournier slowly lifted his Colt. His gun bucked twice as the slugs thumped into Ritter's chest.

8

With glazed eyes and an expression of surprise and anger frozen on his face, Ritter staggered backwards and crashed into the wall behind him. He stood there momentarily, then slowly slid down the wall, leaving a trail of crimson in his wake.

Tournier turned and faced Harding, his Colt levelled at his belly. 'I've decided to forget what you owe me, Harding. Besides, having given the matter more thought, I reckon if I killed you a couple of your old friends from your bounty hunting days might track me down and corner me just for the hell of it.' He lowered his gun. 'I'm not aiming to make trouble for myself so I suggest you stay put 'til I'm long gone. And I'd advise your friends, whoever they are,' he continued, cocking his head in the direction of the approaching horses, 'not to try and follow me.'

Keeping both Harding and the girl covered, he hurried over to Ritter's motionless body and rifled through his pockets. A look of triumph lit his face as he found what he was looking for. He dangled the key in front of his eyes, as if making sure it was the right one.

He looked at Harding, a grin on his face. 'No sense in taking saddle-bags full of money without the key.' He suddenly shot across the room and grabbed hold of Sarah's hair. 'And I'm taking her for safe passage, just in case you and your friends choose to ignore my advice.' A triumphant smile spread across his face. 'I aim to get out of this territory . . . one way or another.'

Harding saw the flash of terror that crossed Sarah's face. She had suffered greatly in the last few days but her ordeal was still not over. Neither could she have any idea how it would end. But the strength and courage Harding saw mirrored in her eyes told him that this was a remarkable woman. A woman any man would be proud to have at his side. And the utter frustration at being unable to do anything to help her out of her continuing predicament made him feel humiliated and worthless.

'Don't try and follow me,' Tournier warned as he yanked at the girl's hair and headed to the door at the side of the shack. 'And if that lot have any sense,' he continued, nodding towards the sound of the horses that were now thundering even closer to the house, 'they'll give up now as well.' With that, he slid out of the side door and, dragging Sarah behind him, made his way to the back of the house.

As soon as they had disappeared out of the door, Harding dashed across the room and retrieved his gun. With expert fingers, he quickly filled the chambers with some of the cartridges that had been discarded on the floor. But by the time the gun had been loaded, he could hear Tournier's horse galloping away in the opposite direction to the approaching riders.

Harding rushed to the door, opened it and fired two shots at the distant cloud of dust that was obscuring his view of Tournier's back. He knew that this was a hollow gesture. He had no chance of reaching Tournier with a Colt at that distance. He returned indoors and slumped into a chair, despair mingled with anger at the knowledge that Sarah was in as much danger as ever.

Seconds later, the door burst open to reveal Deputy Sheriff Colclough and three men. The deputy took one look at Ritter's body and strode over to Harding.

Harding looked up at him. 'Tournier . . . and he's taken the girl as hostage in case we follow him.' He nodded towards the side door. 'He slipped out that way just before you came.'

Colclough grunted.

Harding continued, 'Ritter jumped me when I walked in but he and

Tournier had a little disagreement and that's the result.' He ran his fingers slowly through his hair. 'Tournier's got the money as well.'

Colclough sucked his teeth. 'I came out here today to tell you that we'd reconsidered and decided to help you get this Ritter feller,' he started, 'but I see there's no need now.' He scratched at the brown stubble on his chin and coughed nervously. 'I don't know how to say this other than coming straight out with it . . . so here goes. Ever since you turned up in these parts, mister, all we've had is trouble. Oh, sure, we had some rustling and the occasional bank hold up before you came, but no killings. Now we've lost a sheriff, a mayor and four other folks — Carver, his side-kick, Jenkins and Ritter. You shot two of them and somehow, you've managed to be around when the other two bodies have been found. And although you say a feller named Tournier brought in the first and killed the second, nobody but you has ever seen him. What exactly are you up to, mister?'

Harding raised his eyes and looked directly at the deputy. 'You appear to be accusing me of something. If you are, spit it out.' His voice was calm and cold. 'I've told you the truth. If you choose not to believe me, that's your problem.'

'I'm afraid it's not,' Colclough replied, his face suddenly flushed.

Harding could almost hear the machinations going on inside Colclough's head. He had to find a killer for the sheriff, the mayor and the slaughter of four other men. He knew that Harding had already admitted to the killing of two. Perhaps it wouldn't be so hard to pin the other killings on a man folks in these parts knew nothing much about, except that he had been a bounty hunter.

'Nobody here knows you, Harding. How do we know that you're not responsible for all the killings and Sarah Jenson's kidnapping?'

The expression on Harding's face hardened and his eyes glistened like chips of blue-black ice. 'That's crazy talk!' he spat.

'Maybe, maybe not,' Colclough replied. 'Pass me your Colt. I want to check if it's been fired in the last few minutes.'

'Of course it's been fired,' retorted Harding. 'I loosed off a couple of shots after Tournier.'

'Or maybe there never was any Tournier and you shot Ritter just before we arrived. I heard two shots.' The deputy turned to the others. 'What about you?' They all nodded, some muttering agreement under their breath. 'OK Harding. Hand it over.'

Harding eased his gun out of its holster and passed it on to Colclough, who sniffed the barrel. 'Yup,' he said, eyeing Harding suspiciously. 'It's been fired in the last few minutes, that's for sure.'

'I told you it had been fired,' Harding said coldly.

Colclough placed Harding's gun in his own gun belt. 'I'm going to have to arrest you, feller.' A rumble of agreement ran through the other men at this announcement.

'At least it'll be safe in these parts once we get him behind bars,' one of them muttered to his neighbour out of the side of his mouth.

Without a gun and facing four men, Harding knew it was pointless to resist. 'I've got nothing to hide and I don't aim on running away like some renegade.' He eyed Colclough. 'When Tournier turns up for some more easy pickings in this territory, or when Sarah Jenson's body is found, you'll realize what a bad mistake you've made.'

Colclough grunted something incomprehensible, then jerked his thumb towards the door. 'Your horse out front?'

Harding nodded.

'Right. Saddle up. I'm taking you in.'

Hard riding took them into town within the hour. The jangle of keys and clang of the cell door were familiar sounds to Harding. But the familiarity had come from putting murderers and renegades behind bars. Now, he was having a taste of what he had handed out in the past to all his captives. And he didn't like it. Especially having to share the cells with the two men he had captured after the sheriff's murder. They chuckled quietly as he was put behind bars.

The only piece of furniture in the barren cell was a hard, wooden bunk with two thin, dirty, grey blankets. He stretched out on it, contemplating the mess he was in. As the afternoon shaded into night, he was still wrestling with the dilemma of being accused of the murders that had been committed in the last few days. There was also the likelihood that now he was behind bars, nobody would be out hunting down the real killer. The only consolation was that they would still be looking for Sarah Jenson. Or would they? Nobody had asked him a thing about her. If they thought he was responsible for all the killings, then they must surely think that he had kidnapped Sarah Jenson as well. So why weren't they grilling him?

His thoughts were interrupted by the sound of boots clumping down the wooden corridor leading to the cells. Maybe this was going to be the start of the interrogation. He steeled himself.

9

'OK Harding. On your feet. I want to ask you a couple of questions.' Colclough's voice was heavy with contempt.

'You've got a real bad manner, mister,' Harding replied. 'It'll get you into trouble one day.'

'Listen. I don't have to take that from you. I have a job to do. And part of that job is making sure you swing for the sheriff's murder ... and those of Jenkins and Ritter.'

A cold smile flitted across Harding's face. 'If you and that posse of yours can't do your job properly, it's no reason to make an innocent man swing. I know you must be anxious to find the killer, but this isn't the way to do it.' He smiled coldly. 'What a shame these two hombres aren't awake,' he continued, nodding at the two men he had taken in, 'to hear you saying I'm going to swing for murders I didn't commit.'

Harding saw a flicker of fear cross Colclough's features. 'You seem real anxious to string me up, Colclough.' Harding waited a second or two before adding, 'You never heard of justice?'

The question hit Colclough like a slug in the belly. Momentarily, he seemed to waver and beads of perspiration appeared on his forehead. Then he regained control. 'What the hell are you talking about?' he snarled. His hand grasped his gun, the knuckles showing white with the pressure of the grip.

'You'd never explain away killing me in cold blood, Colclough . . . so you'd better control yourself.'

Sweat began to drip down Colclough's forehead. He stood directly outside Harding's cell, his face a mixture of rage and despair. He breathed deeply and looked down at the floor, his face twitching and his eyes flitting nervously from side to side. Then he grabbed the cell bars. 'You son of a . . . '

Harding saw his chance. Colclough had made the mistake of stepping within his range. Harding's fist shot out between the bars of the cell and flashed towards Colclough's face.

The solid clunk as it connected with Colclough's jaw sent a thrill of anticipation surging through Harding. As Colclough thudded to the floor, Harding knew that he had to find Tournier and bring him back alive if he was to clear himself. He was already labelled a cold-blooded killer. Once they found Colclough laid out on the floor beside the cells, he would be a jail-breaker as well. Then there would be no doubt in the townsfolks' minds about his guilt.

One of the men in the next cell stirred, grunted, then turned over, oblivious to the events that had just taken place. His companion remained on his back, mouth open, snoring loudly.

Harding hauled Colclough's body closer to the bars of the cell and took the bunch of keys that were hanging from his belt. Within seconds, he had opened the cell door and was outside the back door to the sheriff's office. The narrow passage which lay at the back of the office was deserted. He pulled his hat down to shade his face and headed straight for the hitching pole outside the saloon. Picking a horse that looked capable of covering distance at speed, he jumped into the saddle and rode off down the main street. 'Now I'm a horse-thief as well,' he muttered. 'They'll hang me for that alone if I don't find Tournier and bring Sarah back safely.'

Harding didn't waste any time in heading after Tournier. He knew he'd be lucky to catch up with him. But with a woman holding the bounty hunter back and the belief that nobody would be hunting him down, he might not make as fast a pace as he should.

After a hard ride throughout the night, having called in at his own place to pick up some beans, beef, coffee and water, Harding stopped briefly by a small pool of water to give his horse a drink and to refresh himself. He knew that if he was to catch Tournier, he had to ride hard without many breaks.

But after another day's hard riding, he began to think of making camp for the night to give himself and his horse a well-deserved rest. He could still feel a dull ache in his right shoulder and prudence dictated that he rest, if only to ensure that he was fully fit when tackling Tournier. He lit a small fire, brewed some coffee and enjoyed the strong, bitter taste as he swilled it around inside his mouth. After having his fill of beans, he prepared to bed down for the night.

He kicked earth over the last traces of the fire and glanced wistfully at the red ball of fire slowly sinking in the west, wishing he was back on his own ranch with nothing more to trouble him than a couple of broken bob wires. He sighed.

As he was about to take some

blankets off his horse, he was distracted by a small cloud of dust being kicked up in the far distance. He knew they were riders. He just wondered what they were doing in this scrap of hell. He continued watching them and noticed that they were following exactly the same trail as him. They stopped for a couple of minutes, then resumed the trail Harding had left behind. As they got closer, he saw that there were three of them. They stopped again. One man dismounted and examined the ground, whilst his two companions remained on their horses.

Harding saw the man on the ground take off his hat, shield his eyes from the dying rays of the sun and point straight in his direction. In a flash, Harding knew they were tracking him. He had done it himself many times and had no doubt that these men were part of the posse who were hunting him down for what they considered was a whole catalogue of crimes.

As he packed the blanket away again

and picked up the metal cup and plate he had used for his meal, he gave a wry smile. When he had requested volunteers for a posse to hunt down Ritter, not one person had stepped forward. Somehow, Colclough had persuaded another two men to join him on this manhunt. Perhaps they weren't as frightened by his reputation as they had been of Ritter's. Harding smiled grimly. Perhaps they were right to think that. He'd soon have to prove to himself and everybody else that he was still as deadly now as he had been just a couple of years ago.

But nagging doubts about his own ability surfaced when he remembered the run-in he'd had with Ritter and his cronies. He knew he wasn't as fast as he used to be. The question that gnawed away at him was whether he was still fast enough to get Tournier and quick-witted enough to get himself out of the mess he was in.

Harding rode hard that night, having had the benefit of some rest and some food inside him. He wanted to put real distance between himself and the posse, and hopefully, catch up with Tournier at the same time.

Occasionally, his thoughts were filled with memories of his brother. But they were usually displaced by visions of Sarah Jenson. He was not just pursuing Tournier to clear his name. His other motive was as old as mankind. He had seen a woman of beauty and refinement. A woman that he would be proud to have as his wife.

Through a cruel twist of fate, she had been robbed of the man she was to marry. Now, if he saved her, he would have as good a chance as any man to make her his wife. Not because he saved her. But because of the flickering fire he was sure he'd seen in her eyes when they had first met. A meeting that now seemed an eternity ago.

His enforced stay in the saddle was something Harding was no longer used to. Although he knew he had to keep moving, his body ached for rest. The pain in his shoulder was getting worse as he pushed his tired body to keep going, but he dare not stop, not knowing how hungry his pursuers were to catch him.

So absorbed had Harding become at putting as much distance between himself and the men chasing him that it was with a sense of surprise that he suddenly realized his quarry was within sight. The two figures in front of him, heading directly for the border, could only be Tournier and Sarah. Nobody else would have any reason for riding in this godforsaken country. Only the hunters and the hunted.

All Harding's old instincts came flooding back. It was as if he had never stopped being a bounty hunter. He became much more careful in tracking them now that he had them in his sights. Once, using the stealth that had been so valuable when he had done this kind of work for a living, he got close enough to spot the red of Sarah Jenson's shirt and the gold of her long, flowing hair. Up until that moment, there had been a fragment of doubt in his mind that he had been following somebody else. Now, there was absolutely no doubt.

His body ached with tiredness and pain but he hardly noticed. The excitement of the chase and the anticipation of action coursed through his blood. If only Sarah knew that he was close by . . . but there was no way he could let her know until he made his play. Until then, she'd simply have to endure whatever horrors Tournier was forcing on her. Just for a few more hours.

It was night before Harding moved closer. Dismounting, he padded the hooves of his horse with strips torn from his blanket, then quietly led it up a steep, rocky incline so that he could have a better view of Tournier's movements. At first, the horse was reluctant to climb, but Harding's gentle coaxing finally managed to get it up to the rim of a ridge which overlooked

Tournier's camp for the night.

Harding tied the horse to one of the birches nearby, then lay down on the edge of the ridge to keep guard.

Harding could barely distinguish what Tournier was saying to the girl when he spoke to her. A wind had suddenly whipped up, and it seemed to carry the sounds of Tournier's voice away from him. It was apparent, however, that Sarah was refusing to talk to him. On occasions, Tournier became angry and raised his voice loud enough for Harding to hear. 'I asked you how you were feeling,' he snapped.

Harding saw the girl look at her captor with sullen indifference. 'Not that you care,' she replied bitterly, 'but I'm as well as can be expected bearing in mind the company I'm keeping.'

Tournier threw the remains of his coffee on the fire, snorting in exasperation. 'Better watch that mouth of yours, lady. It's going to get you into trouble.'

'You mean this is not trouble?' she

asked incredulously, as if poking fun at him.

Tournier snorted again in a mixture of annoyance and exasperation, as if not knowing how to deal with this spirited woman. As he looked down at her, seeing her eyes glaring defiantly at Tournier, Harding thought what a courageous young woman she was. Alone and defenceless, she was still standing up to the man who had captured her.

Perhaps she's given up all hope of being rescued and expects the worst, Harding mused. Showing her courage and responding with dignity to prevent Tournier having the pleasure of seeing her beaten and humiliated. He took off his stetson and ran his fingers through his hair. A real strong filly, he thought.

Having decided not to make his move until later on that evening, when Tournier was asleep, Harding stood up and crept stealthily back towards his horse. He hauled the remains of the blanket he had torn off the animal's back and wrapped it around his shoulders to keep himself warm.

'Whoa, boy,' he whispered reassuringly. 'You just stand real still and stay real quiet.'

Harding gingerly picked his way back towards his vantage point. He knew that there were some loose rocks under his feet and he didn't want to disturb any in case they alerted Tournier. Even worse, they could crash down the rock face to where Tournier was sitting. Harding wanted to pick his own time to tackle Tournier and this was not it.

As he lay down once more, blinking momentarily as he tried to focus in the dark, he felt a sudden chill run down his spine. It was a well-developed sixth sense that had served him well in the past and it suddenly seemed to be warning him again. In years gone by, he hadn't minded the strange, cold feeling of impending danger. Back then, it had been displaced by a surge of excitement and power at the conflict to come. But now, all Harding could feel was a continuous chill of impending panic that seeped into his bones and hit him in the pit of his stomach.

'Move one inch, feller, and I'll blow your head off.' Harding judged that the man who had spoken was around ten feet away. He recognized the voice as that of Tournier.

Harding knew that although Tournier hadn't recognized him, or even suspected that it might be him, the moment he turned around to face him, Tournier would blast him to hell. He was a man who would not take kindly to being tracked, especially by a man who had been warned off.

'Take that gun out of your holster . . . real slow . . . throw it across to the side, then stand up.'

Harding did as he was told.

'Turn around so's I can get a look at you.'

Harding turned round to face Tournier. All he could see was a silhouette several feet away from him. He couldn't recognize Tournier and he was certain that Tournier couldn't recognize him.

'I'm sorry, mister,' Harding lied, his voice deliberately disguised with a quiver. 'I just saw the fire and smelt the cooking so I thought I'd try to join you . . . I'm real hungry . . . haven't eaten for two days.' Harding carried on babbling. 'Ran out of food and water and I haven't been able . . . '

'OK feller,' Tournier interrupted sharply. 'I don't need your whole life story.' He walked across to where Harding had thrown his gun and picked it up. 'I'll keep this for safe keeping for the time being.' He stuffed the gun into his belt. 'Just walk down in front of me and I'll see what I can rustle up for you . . . and then you're on your way out of here. You understand me, feller?'

'Sure,' Harding mumbled, lowering his face. He could see Tournier's gun trained on him. He feverishly searched his mind for a way out of this dilemma before Tournier discovered his true identity. If he didn't recognize him on the way down to the camp-fire, Sarah certainly would the moment she saw him. And it would be too much to expect her not to show some sign of relief or emotion after the trauma she'd been through.

Harding clambered down the steep incline keeping at least three feet ahead of Tournier. It was dark and treacherous. On two occasions, he lost his footing. 'Come on, feller,' growled the exasperated voice behind him. 'You can't be that hungry that you're so weak you're falling all over the place.'

'Sorry, mister. It's kinda dark. Can't see which way I'm going.'

Shortly afterwards, Harding approached the glow of light thrown out by the fire. He could see Sarah, huddled close to the fire, arms wrapped tightly around herself to keep warm and protect herself from the chill wind that had suddenly arisen. She looked around as the two men approached, then returned her attention to the fire.

'There's some coffee for you there,

feller. I'll get you some beans and stuff . . . ' Tournier was not even looking at Harding as he spoke.

As Harding came into the girl's view, she glanced up at him. A small, stifled cry escaped her lips, attracting Tournier's attention. His black eyes flashed towards Harding.

For the merest fraction of a second, their eyes locked, then Tournier's hand flashed towards his gun. Harding lunged at him, one hand preventing Tournier from drawing, the other smashing into his face. The gun dropped to the ground as Tournier fumbled his grip and he gave a grunt of pain as Harding's clenched fist thumped into his mouth.

Both men tumbled to the ground, raising a cloud of dust. Harding heard another stifled cry from Sarah as he leapt to his feet. Knowing no quarter would be asked for or given in this fight, which he instinctively knew would be to the death, he aimed a kick at Tournier's head. As his boot was about to crash into Tournier's face, Harding saw his opponent's leg whip up viciously beneath him. The iron-tipped cap of Tournier's boot flashed in the light of the fire before Harding felt an agonizing pain explode in his groin. He gave an anguished cry. His eyes began to water. Brilliant blue, black and silver stars erupted before his eyes. He crumpled to the ground, his head slumped forward.

Another vicious kick to the side of the head sent him reeling, and more bright lights cascaded before his eyes. He dragged air into his lungs in long, shuddering breaths.

Tournier was by now searching the ground for the gun he had dropped earlier. Harding hauled himself to his feet, his body shaking with weakness after the blows that had landed on him. He felt stabs of pain shooting through his wounded right arm, the force of the blow he had smashed into Tournier's face having jarred it.

He staggered over to Tournier, who

was still scrabbling about in the dust and half darkness for his gun. Harding drew back his foot and gave him a powerful kick to the side. He heard a whoosh of air escape from Tournier's lungs, followed by what sounded like the cry of a wounded animal. Tournier turned on him, his face etched with the pain of the kick Harding had landed as well as a mixture of hate and fear at the conflict he was now engaged in. It was as if he also knew that only one of them would be alive after this battle.

Head bent low, Tournier charged Harding, catching him in the midriff. Already stunned by the earlier blows, Harding had no time to get out of the way of the charge and felt himself being carried along by the other man's momentum. As he careered backwards, his feet stumbled on some rocks and he fell, Tournier crashing down on top of him.

Every bone in Harding's body was jarred by the fall. Momentarily he was winded, all the air in his lungs having been expelled by the force of the fall. Dragging on some cold night air, he attempted to push Tournier off him. But Tournier would have none of it. He clung on tenaciously, pinning Harding to the ground.

Harding wondered what advantage this could possibly gain Tournier when he felt a searing pain in his right ear. Tournier had grabbed it between his teeth. Harding gave a yelp of pain as he felt teeth biting deep into his flesh. With his right hand, he pushed hard against Tournier's face and searched out his eyes. If his opponent was going to fight dirty, then there was no reason why he shouldn't do the same. Finding the soft fleshy eyes of his opponent, he jabbed a thumb into one of them with vicious intent. The clamp of teeth around his ear loosened as a scream rent the air.

Harding took his chance. He shoved Tournier away from him, then struggled to his feet, feeling his ear. It was gushing blood, but he had no time to dwell on his wounds. He looked up as he heard the other man coming at him again, his mouth spattered with blood and murder in his eyes. He threw a right fist at Harding's jaw. Harding blocked it with his arm. But no sooner had he blocked that blow than another fist crashed into the side of his head, pounding his already bloodied ear and making his senses whirl again. He stumbled under the force of the blow but did not fall. Expecting another fist to come crashing into him, he swayed to one side, hoping it would miss him.

But no fist came. Instead, it was another vicious kick to his groin that followed. The blinding pain he had felt earlier was redoubled. His already throbbing groin was ill prepared for another assault and he cried out in agony as the blow hit him. A wave of nausea gripped him. He crouched down, desperately seeking some relief from the pain that engulfed his whole being. But there was no escape. Only another barrage of blows to the head which felled him to the ground.

Through the dim light thrown on the two of them by the fire, Harding saw that Tournier was once again searching for his gun. The moment he found it, Harding knew he'd be shot dead. At all costs, he had to stop Tournier finding it. Then he remembered seeing Tournier discarding the gun he had confiscated from him when he had approached the fire. It was also fully loaded. Either would be sufficient for Tournier to blow him to hell and back.

Harding felt a breeze of fresh, cold air fan his face. He breathed in deeply, then hauled himself to his feet. He half stumbled, half ran over to where Tournier was frantically raking the ground with his hands. A look of panic and desperation creased Tournier's features. On all fours, he was scrabbling around like a chicken searching out scraps of food in a yard. Only he looked a great deal less dignified. Scrabbling in the dirt comes naturally to a chicken or a hog. It does not come naturally to a bounty hunter. But without his gun, it was what Tournier was reduced to. A pathetic sight, rather than the fearsome one he presented when a gun was slung low on his hip or cradled in the palm of his hand.

Using the momentum built up from his lumbering run, Harding smashed a kick into Tournier's face, to great effect. As his boot connected with Tournier's head, its thud was accompanied by the sound of bone cracking. Tournier gave another howl of anguish as he crashed sideways. Blood poured from his nose. It had been severely damaged by Harding's kick and appeared to be broken.

Harding took heart when he saw Tournier's face. Although he was in considerable pain himself, both from the blows Tournier had landed and from the wound in his right arm, he could see that Tournier was in even worse shape. Perhaps the presence of a gun close to hand had prevented Tournier from becoming an accomplished fist fighter. Whatever the reason, it seemed to Harding that the bounty hunter was completely out of his depth when standing man to man with nothing to call on but his two fists.

Harding stared hard into Tournier's eyes. He wanted to know if Tournier was beginning to doubt that he could beat him. Whether the mirrors of the man's soul could tell him if Tournier was contemplating defeat. But all Harding could see was the blaze of anger and pain. Tournier charged at him again, arms flailing and head bent low to catch Harding in the stomach.

Harding stood his ground until Tournier was just two feet away from him, then stepped nimbly aside. At the same time, he raised his right foot and swung it round to catch Tournier's head as he charged past. The impact caused a shock wave to travel through Harding's body. Tournier crumpled to the ground once more, then slowly stood up, shaking his head. The glazed look in his eyes reflected a mixture of pain, puzzlement and bewilderment.

With a roar of defiance and anger, he came at Harding again. But this time he advanced more cautiously, eyeing Harding warily as he approached him. Harding waited for him to make his next move. He didn't want to expend any more energy than was necessary because he was already beginning to feel his strength ebbing away. The long, hard journey tracking down Tournier and the combined effects of the gunshot wound and Tournier's blows were definitely having a debilitating effect on him.

Tournier moved towards him slowly, then suddenly lashed out with his right fist. Harding stepped back. As he did so, he tripped on a rock, and sprawled on to his back. Tournier wasted no time. He lunged towards him and drew his leg back to throw a heavy kick at Harding's side. Harding managed to grab it before it reached him. He twisted Tournier's foot around sharply and yanked hard. Offbalance, Tournier tumbled to the ground, his twisted ankle still held firmly in Harding's grip. Harding scrambled to his feet and, still holding Tournier's foot, planted a savage kick in his groin.

The shock that Harding's kick caused to his senses seemed to give Tournier an added strength and an increased determination to overcome his opponent. Despite his outraged scream of pain, he immediately jumped to his feet and landed a solid blow to Harding's mouth.

Harding, surprised at this sudden ferocity, felt the salty taste of his own blood filling his mouth. He licked his lips with his tongue to find that they had been split open with the ferocity of Tournier's blow.

For a moment, Harding felt his resolve weaken. This was reinforced when a shuddering left fist to the throat caused him to choke and gasp for air. He felt consciousness slipping away from him and a thick grey mist swam before his eyes. He tried to heave some air into his lungs through what he now guessed to be a damaged windpipe. His eyes watered heavily and his heart pounded to a degree he hadn't felt since the danger he had experienced three years earlier on the Roberts hunt. That hunt had been the first in a line of events that had persuaded him to quit when he still had relative youth on his side and the health to enjoy life. Now he found himself in a situation where there was a clear danger he would never embark on that life.

Tournier had seen the damage caused by his first attack to Harding's neck and wasn't about to give up such an advantage easily. A further vicious blow to the throat sent Harding reeling backwards. He clawed desperately at his damaged neck.

He tumbled to the ground, still blinded by the tears that poured from his eyes as the choking that had begun with the first blow was exacerbated by the second.

For several seconds, Harding lay on the ground, coughing and wheezing as he tried to overcome the deadly effects of his opponent's latest attack. Then he felt a fiery pain searing at his back and shoulders and the acrid smell of burning flesh and hair filled his nostrils. His hand automatically left his throat and grabbed the back of his shoulder.

To his horror, Harding saw flames licking at his jacket. His hair was already singed by the flames and he felt a seizure of panic as his trousers suddenly caught fire, the flames being fanned by the stiff breeze. He uttered a cry of alarm when he saw the cause of his discomfort. He had stumbled backwards and fallen directly on to the camp-fire he had seen Tournier and Sarah sitting around only minutes earlier.

He rolled away from the fire but to no avail. Both his jacket and trousers had caught fire and they were beginning to burn fiercely.

Blind panic seized Harding. Ever since he had seen his parents' barn burn down as a child, frying to death three cattle and his beloved dog, he had felt an irrational terror of raging, uncontrolled flames.

Others had their own fears. Some would shake at the sight and sound of a rattlesnake. Others feared the bloodcurdling whoop of redskins on the warpath. And he had once met a man whose sole fear in life was the dread of falling asleep because he feared he would never wake again. But for Harding, it was the terrible scenes of his childhood that had formed his greatest fear.

Desperately rolling around on the earth to try and extinguish the flames, Harding had lost all concern with Tournier's next move. But he did hear a distant voice shouting at him through the agony of intense heat blistering his skin and singeing the hair on his head.

'Burn in hell, Harding. Maybe I'll see you there sometime.'

With those words ringing in his ears, Harding continued rolling in the dirt. He grabbed handfuls of earth and threw them over himself to douse the flames. But he was weakening.

The combined effects of the punishment meted out to him by Tournier, the lack of air he could drag into his lungs and the intense pain he was experiencing at being burnt alive made him sob with despair.

The sound of a pair of horses galloping away was only a minor distraction to the fight he now had on his hands. A fight to survive.

10

The acrid smell of burning flesh filled
Harding's nostrils, almost choking him.
He screamed in anguish as the flames
began to engulf him. From the deep
recesses of his mind came the shrill cry
for self-preservation. In response, he
managed to drag his body off the
ground, desperately searching for a
small gully or hollow that would
contain enough sand or loose dirt that
he could throw over himself to extinguish the flames.

He staggered aimlessly for a few
yards, still screaming in agony at the
pain searing through his flesh and his
senses. Never had he felt such agony.
Even when that crazy old Sioux had cut
a slug out of his shoulder and
cauterized it with a red-hot iron, the
pain hadn't been this bad.

He fell to his knees, a wave of nausea

washing over him. Suddenly, he felt very tired. Shaking his head, he struggled to remain conscious, knowing that the fingers of death were beckoning him. He fought against the waves of pain and tiredness that swept over him. Fought like he had never fought before.

He scrambled to his feet again, but his legs collapsed beneath him, defying all his efforts to rise again. He fell to his side and for a moment almost blacked out, succumbing to the intense pain that was now invading his whole being. But the movement of his body falling down a steep ridge kept him conscious.

For a few seconds, Harding felt as if he was floating on air. Then the jolt of his body thudding into the ground after falling down into a ravine shook him awake. Even as he began choking on the dust disturbed by his fall, he knew that it could save him if he retained the will to fight on.

With skin dripping off his hands, he began to shower himself with dirt and sand. He rolled over and over in the dust, desperately trying to extinguish the fire that had turned him into a human torch. After two minutes of frantic activity, the flames had gone, leaving behind smoking clothes and the sickly smell of burnt flesh.

Harding lay on the ground, sucking the cold night air into his parched and scorched lungs. He could see the stars glittering in the black sky above and feel the dampness of the earth beneath his head and body. He breathed erratically, his tortured limbs shuddering with pain every few seconds. The badly burnt flesh on his hands, face and back throbbed incessantly.

He remained there for over half an hour, simply gazing up at the black sky, thinking, hearing and seeing nothing. Just to survive was enough.

Gradually, the pain began to ease. He struggled to his feet and scrambled up to where he had fought with Tournier. He wanted to find his own gun and Tournier's. Although his mind was intent on pursuing the only man who could prove his innocence if captured alive, his body rebelled against the idea. But then the thought of Sarah Jenson flashed into his mind, reminding him that proving his innocence was only part of it. Tournier was despoiling a young life. And that could not be allowed to continue.

Harding spent twenty minutes painstakingly searching the ground before he found the two guns. He slipped his own gun into its holster and stuck Tournier's into his belt after checking that both were loaded with five slugs each. If nothing else, he and Tournier had the same habit of having one empty chamber in their guns.

He climbed slowly back to the top of the ridge and breathed a sigh of relief at the sight of his horse waiting patiently for him. He was still suffering the ill effects of the smoke he had inhaled and the climb left him breathless and gasping, like an old man. He sat down for another few minutes before swinging into the saddle.

As the horse slowly cantered along in the direction Tournier had taken, Harding gingerly felt his face, hair and eyebrows. His eyebrows had been singed and completely burnt off and patches of his hair felt brittle and powdery. But he took some comfort from the fact that his face appeared to be relatively unaffected. It was his hands that had suffered the most.

Gritting his teeth, he resolved to take alive the man who was responsible for putting him through this agony. His old professionalism returned with a vengeance as he headed after Tournier, blocking out the pain that still engulfed his body. It was there, but he would not let if affect him. He had a job to do. And he was going to do it.

He headed towards the border. If Tournier has any sense, Harding figured, that's where he'll head. And Tournier had plenty of sense. Cunning too. And deadly quick reflexes that had left many a man breathing their last into the dirt of dozens of towns throughout the West.

But the exhaustion that was now beginning to grip Harding, in addition to the pain of the battle with Tournier and the effects of the fire, did not shake his resolve. He knew what he had to do. If he failed the only thing that would welcome him back to Sentenas was the hangman's noose.

He had been riding slowly for almost an hour when the reverberations of a distant crack of gunfire made him sit up sharply on his horse. It was still dark, although the plain ahead of him was bathed in silvery moonlight. He reined in his horse and sat still for several seconds but no other sound broke the silence that enveloped the plain.

Harding guessed that the only person who could have fired that shot was Tournier . . . or possibly Sarah Jenson. He felt a thrill of excitement coursing through him as he realized that he was definitely on their trail. Whatever had caused that shot to be fired had confirmed to him that he was on the right track.

It was approaching sun-up when Harding saw the tiny puff of dust way ahead of him, drifting closer and closer to the mountains that had to be negotiated by anyone who wanted to cross the border. To his surprise, he noticed that he was getting closer to Tournier. The reason for that became clear when he came across the carcass of Sarah's horse. It had a broken leg and had been shot in the head to put it out of its misery.

Harding knew then that Tournier would have to sit it out and fight with him. There was no way he'd get to the border on one horse if two people were riding it. Either he'd have to drop Sarah . . . or kill her, or he'd have to ride so slowly that Harding would easily catch up with them. His only real alternative, thought Harding, if he wants to get to the border in one piece with all his money, is to pick a good spot to bushwhack me.

Harding grinned at the dilemma Tournier found himself in. 'So near and yet so far,' he murmured.

Knowing that Tournier would try and pick him off if he continued travelling in a straight line and came within range of whatever rifle he was carrying, Harding made a sharp detour to the north. After a few minutes hard riding, he swung towards the mountains again. He figured he could get up the mountain almost as fast as Tournier. Once at the top, he'd pin Tournier down before the bounty hunter had a chance to cross the range and head towards the safety of the border.

'Even if he crosses that border, it won't stop me going after him,' vowed Harding. 'If he thinks it's going to be that easy getting away from me . . . ' Harding grinned again, feeling more confident about his chances of capturing Tournier despite the vicious pains still enveloping his body.

He scrambled across the rocks at the base of the mountains. At the foothills, he took a firm hold of his horse's reins and slowly started climbing, dragging the horse behind him. After pulling the reluctant animal for about a hundred yards, Harding realized that he had to either tether the beast and finish the journey to the summit on his own, or forget about pursuing Tournier.

Minutes later, after having safely secured the horse to a large tree-stump until his eventual return, Harding clambered up the steep mountain face.

Occasionally he glanced across to see how Tournier and Sarah were progressing. Although he knew that Tournier must have spotted him by now, the bounty hunter had the added problem of not being able to leave his horse behind. There was no way he'd get to the border without it, so he had to drag it up the mountain with him, along with a reluctant hostage.

Harding grinned as he saw the difficulty Tournier was having. He kept well out of rifle range in case Tournier decided to take a shot at him. But he ensured that he kept them in his sights at all time.

Harding reached the summit a good twenty minutes before Tournier. He sat down and lit a smoke, pondering what to do next. It was all too easy to wait for Tournier to get near the summit and start taking pot-shots at him. Easy and stupid. Because all he'd do was grab Sarah and threaten to blow her head off.

No, thought Harding. What I'll do is work out where they're going to reach the top, find a little hole where I won't be spotted and pick him off cleanly. Just enough to wind him. Because he's no use to me dead, even if that would mean Sarah going free.

Harding knew the risks he was taking. Not only for himself but for Sarah. Tournier was less than useless to him dead. But if he wounded him seriously, he might die before he could talk to the deputy and the townsfolk, thereby preventing Harding from proving his innocence. If the wound was superficial, Tournier would have the chance to grab Sarah and do as he wished with her. Under those circumstances, he would be able to keep Harding at bay for as long as he wanted. Probably all the way to the border.

Harding took a long drag of the smoke he held tightly between his teeth, then spat it out. He had no option but to try and temporarily disable him. He couldn't just let Tournier ride for the border with Sarah and the money, to say nothing of the alibi that he needed so desperately himself.

Harding crouched low as he ran along the top of the mountain range, gritting his teeth at the pain that still racked his body. He had a fair idea where the two of them would surface and he wanted to be waiting for them. Knowing that Tournier would be expecting him to lie in ambush, Harding imagined what he would do if he was in the other man's boots.

He reckoned that he knew Tournier

well enough to figure out that he would certainly use Sarah as some kind of shield when they topped the ridge. Somehow, he had to find a hiding place that would be out of Tournier's sight but would also give him a clear view of Sarah and her captor when they appeared.

There was no such spot. He had to settle for a large boulder that afforded protection but very little opportunity for seeing who was approaching without peering around it and exposing himself. He had to rely on hearing them. Not the most satisfactory way of trying to ambush an outlaw. But the only way open to him.

Harding leant against the rock, the Winchester he had picked up at the shack cradled in his right arm, listening intently for the slightest sound. For a long time, all he heard was the wind rustling through some dried, decaying vegetation and the far off howling of coyotes.

Suddenly, he heard a man swearing.

Harding stiffened. He couldn't believe that Tournier didn't know he was waiting for him. And knowing that, why was he making enough noise to wake up those planted in Boot Hill?

Harding glanced quickly around the rock. To his astonishment, he saw Sarah Jenson standing alone at the top of the ridge just twenty yards away from him. For a second, he didn't understand what was happening. Where was Tournier? Why weren't they together?

Then the spattering of splintered rock against his face gave him the answer. Tournier had tricked him into showing himself. Obviously, when Tournier had reached the top of the mountain, he had shoved Sarah into full view of Harding, taken cover himself and then caused enough disturbance to let Harding think it was safe to break cover.

'Damn,' swore Harding. 'Now he knows exactly where I am.' He loosed off a couple of shots in the general direction that Tournier's shots had come from, but he knew that he was firing wildly with no chance of hitting him. His opportunity of taking Tournier by surprise had gone. He cursed again at his own stupidity.

He glanced around the other side of the rock to see if Sarah was still in view. As he'd expected, she'd gone, no doubt ordered back by Tournier so that he could use her again as a decoy if he needed to.

Harding reloaded his Winchester and checked his Colt. He also checked Tournier's gun, then stuffed it back into his belt. The nagging worry that he might soon run out of ammunition concentrated his mind. He had to get Tournier as quickly as possible, using as few slugs as possible.

Beads of sweat formed on his forehead and began to trickle down the side of his face. He wiped them away with the palm of his right hand. He could see his problems mounting and that made him very uncomfortable.

He drew a deep breath. Taking off his

hat, he stuck it out just a fraction on the right side of the rock to see how well placed Tournier was. There was no reaction. But when he repeated the same exercise on the other side, it was instant. A bullet tore straight through his hat and almost ripped it out of his hand. Replacing it on his head, Harding now knew from which side he could make his break.

He took another deep breath. He had to do something. From where he was presently hiding, he judged the distance to the next rock to be some ten yards. If he reached it, he might have a better chance of spotting where Tournier was hiding and flush him out. Despite the aching in his limbs and the burning sensations in his shoulders and hands, he fired off another couple of shots from his Colt to distract Tournier's attention. Then, weaving crazily, he made for the rock to his right.

Bullets thudded into the ground beside him as he staggered towards the rock and dirt spat into his face as the force of the slugs shattered the ground around him. He threw himself to the ground behind the rock. His bones jarred as he hit the hard, solid ground. He took a few moments to recover his breath before checking that his guns were still in his holster and stuck into his belt.

If he had any advantage over Tournier it was the fact that he had two hand-guns rather than the rifle Tournier was using. He also had a Winchester, but it was cumbersome for close fighting, especially when trying to gain advantage by sprinting from rock to rock to try and surprise your opponent or to get a better vantage point.

Clenching his teeth, Harding rolled over on to his belly and dug his elbows into the ground. Then he edged forward and peered out cautiously from behind the rock. Instead of bullets spitting into the ground, which was what he expected, he heard Tournier calling him.

'Show yourself, Harding, or I'll kill the girl.'

Harding stiffened. For a moment, he didn't know how to respond. He moistened his lips with his tongue. 'You won't do that. You'd never sink as low as Ritter. He'd kill her . . . but not you. You just want her to make sure you have safe passage to the border.'

Silence engulfed the range. Only the whistling of the wind and the rustle of some dried weeds broke the silence.

Harding felt his heart thumping dangerously, uncertain as to how Tournier would react to what he had said.

'You're right. I wouldn't harm a woman. That's not my style.'

'So release her.'

'Nope. As you say, I need her for safe passage. Once I've killed you there may be others behind you. They might not read me as well as you do, Harding. They're just plain folk. If I threaten to kill the girl, they'll believe me, so she stays with me.'

Even before he had finished, the morning air cracked with the sound of two more bullets being fired. One thumped into the dirt only a foot away from Harding and the other smashed into the top of the rock, causing more splinters to shower down on him.

Harding returned fire immediately, almost emptying his Colt at the rock he now knew Tournier to be hiding behind. If there was one thing he didn't want Tournier to even begin to suspect, it was that he was rapidly running out of ammunition.

As soon as the last shot was fired, Harding made another dash to a nearby rock. He wanted to get as close as possible to Tournier to see if he was using, or would use, Sarah as a shield when things hotted up.

He also wanted to take him alive. And the closer he was to him, the easier it would be to wound Tournier rather than kill him. But everything depended on the element of surprise. He cursed again for having been fooled so easily by his opponent. It would now be doubly difficult, almost impossible, to surprise Tournier.

As he wrestled with his predicament, he heard the crack of another rifle shot and instinctively ducked. But this time there was no splintering of rock or spitting of dust around him.

Another couple of shots rang out, then Harding heard loud cursing coming from Tournier's direction. Puzzled, Harding immediately poked his head out to see what was going on. He was just in time to see a distant figure, crouching beside a rock, taking aim and firing directly at where Tournier and the girl were hiding.

Harding's blood ran cold when he heard Sarah's terrified screams as the bullet smashed into the boulder above her head. 'What the . . . ' he began, then watched with a mixture of horror and bewilderment as another two men, close to the original gunman, appeared in view and took a couple of shots at Tournier.

For a moment, Harding remained motionless, trying to figure out what was happening. But revulsion engulfed him when he realized that the gunmen had started firing indiscriminately, caring little for a woman's presence.

A chill ran through Harding's body at the thought of the danger Sarah was in. He was about to break cover when he heard Tournier returning fire and then running towards his horse. He had obviously decided that the only way to escape was to get to his horse and make a getaway, without the girl, who would only slow him down.

He was only feet away from his horse when the bullet hit him. He spun around, arms flailing in the air. Then he crashed to the ground. He remained motionless as more shots spattered into the dust around him.

Whoever these guys are . . . and it can only be Colclough and his cronies, reasoned Harding, they certainly want to finish him off. They sure as hell have no intention of taking him alive.

The thought had not been lost on him that if they behaved like this with

Tournier, he himself could expect similar treatment. He watched Tournier drag himself towards the cover of a small crop of rocks.

Harding decided that there was only one way to save the girl. The gunmen were still pouring lead around the area where Tournier was hiding. And Sarah was still crouched behind a boulder only a couple of yards away from him. It would only be a matter of time before she was hit. Harding broke cover, took careful aim and fired a couple of shots from his Winchester at the men's position.

Fire being returned from someone other than Tournier must have stunned them because a long silence followed with no retaliation. Harding stumbled towards the boulder behind which Tournier had crawled. It was in his interests to keep Tournier alive and he had no intention of letting Colclough blast him to hell before he could get him to admit his part in the affairs of the last few days.

When he reached Tournier he knew that his chances of getting him to talk, never mind helping him out of a tight spot, were nil. Blood was oozing out of a gaping hole in his side and dribbling out of his mouth. His eyes had a glazed look. When Harding looked into them, all he could see was the shadow of death.

'You're dying, Tournier . . . and you know it. Tell me why Ritter hired you and what this is all about.'

Tournier's eyes focused on Harding, then drifted away over his shoulder, a faraway look in them. As if making a supreme effort, he opened his mouth. But no words came out. Then his head rolled sideways.

At that precise moment, more shots splattered into the ground, one of them coming uncomfortably close to Harding. He hugged the rock, gaining as much shelter as he could, wondering what Tournier had been about to tell him.

Harding glanced across at Sarah. He

could see her cowering against a bank of earth adjacent to the rock behind which she and Tournier had been hiding earlier. Her face was ghostly white. She saw Harding looking at her. Suddenly, she sprang to her feet and ran towards him.

Before she had covered three yards, bullets began spitting into the ground around her. Harding watched in horror as she staggered towards him, then fell in a hail of gunfire. As she lay on the ground, more bullets thumped into her body, which jerked violently as they hit her.

11

The full impact of what he had just witnessed took a few moments to dawn on Harding. The sight of Sarah's prone body, spreadeagled in the dirt, was such a shock that he was unable to react.

Then, with an angry growl, he opened fire indiscriminately at the position of the men who had shot her down. Under cover of his own fire, both guns blazing, smoking, he sprinted towards her and managed to pull her behind a rock.

As he slumped down behind the boulder, exhausted by the tension of the last few minutes, a volley of slugs thumped into the ground close to him. But at that moment, Harding had more urgent matters to attend to.

He took Sarah Jenson in his arms and looked into her face. Her eyes were closed and the expression on her face was as if she was peacefully asleep. But a sudden foreboding set Harding's heart pounding uncontrollably.

Her body had been hit three times. He could see no presence of a pulse in her neck. With a mounting sense of alarm, he lifted her arm and felt for some sign of a pulse in her wrist. There was none. And there was not the slightest breath of life coming from her mouth or nose.

Harding smoothed back the strands of golden hair that had fallen across her face, marvelling at the beauty that was now lost to him forever. He drew her hard against his chest and cradled her in his arms for a few moments, mourning the loss of his chance for happiness.

Then he laid her down on the ground, his mind still stunned at the suddenness and ferocity of her murder. Coming on top of everything else that had happened to him, this latest twist of fate was a very bitter blow.

The sound of a familiar voice shouting

instructions pierced his numbed, grief-stricken brain. He recognized the voice of Deputy Sheriff Colclough. He was ordering his men to circle around behind Harding to trap him.

A cold black anger began churning in Harding's belly. His heart and mind cried out for revenge against the men who had orchestrated the brutal and needless murder of an innocent young woman. The fact that she had also been the woman he loved added fire to the rage that writhed and boiled inside him.

He reloaded his two hand-guns and Winchester with speed and cold efficiency. Inwardly seething, but outwardly calm, he readied himself for a fight that would see him either dead or hanged, or a similar fate befalling the men he was about to face.

Harding broke cover again, guns blazing. This time his shooting was more controlled and aimed directly at any man who showed himself. Pinning them down, he managed to get close to the man who had tried to outflank him on the left. He ran towards the rock where the man was hiding. Most of his fire was now aimed at preventing his opponent from loosing off any more shots.

He was almost on top of him when the man broke cover. The gunman glanced back over his shoulder at Harding to reveal a terror-stricken expression on his face. 'No . . . I'll talk,' he shouted as he saw Harding bear down on him. 'It's Colclough's fault . . . '

But Harding was in no mood to talk. The bloodied image of Sarah Jenson was still emblazoned on his mind. 'Fight,' he snarled, his smoking guns levelled at the man's chest as he stormed towards him. The terrified man swung his Winchester half-heartedly towards Harding, as if he knew that an attempt to fight such a man would be futile.

It was. Harding loosed off two shots that struck the man in the chest, immediately causing a huge stain of red to spread across his shirt and his body to be hurled violently back against the rocks.

Messy business, thought Harding, congratulating himself on the fact that his old skills of hunting, ferreting out and killing were still intact.

The elation that surged through his body at the kill was again replaced by cold efficiency as he turned his attention back to the task in hand.

'Stay and fight,' Harding heard Colclough shout. 'I'll blow your head off if you run out on me.'

Harding could hardly hear the other man's reply but this was academic because he saw Colclough's companion swing onto his horse.

What followed next suddenly caused all the doubts and suspicions about the events of the last few days to slip neatly into place in Harding's mind. At last he had the solution to certain inconsistencies that had puzzled him. They had seemed completely unrelated, but now he understood.

Colclough turned his gun on the man

who was riding out and shot him in the back. The man slid from his saddle and crashed to the ground.

'Colclough,' Harding shouted. 'Either you throw down your gun or I'm coming after you.'

Colclough gave a harsh laugh. 'I've never thrown down my gun, Harding. So you'll just have to come and get me. I'll take great pleasure in blowing you to hell, the same as I have with all the others.'

Harding crouched behind a rock and reloaded. He figured that Colclough would fight. He knew the man had no option. After sliding five slugs into his own Colt, he began to reload the gun he had picked up the previous night after the fight with Tournier.

Concern furrowed his brow as he saw that he had only three slugs left. He looked at Tournier's prostrate body and figured that if he could reach the dead man's gun belt, he'd be OK. But he'd have to use all his remaining ammunition as cover to get it. And there was no certainty that there were any slugs left in the belt. After all, Tournier had thrown a lot of lead around in the last half an hour.

Harding knew that he had no option but to get to the gun belt. Eight slugs and two in the Winchester wouldn't get him very far with a man like Colclough if there was going to be a long, drawn out gun battle. Colclough might be evil but he was no fool. He'd fight to the bitter end and use all the tricks and experience he had gained through his dubious career as a lawman.

Harding loosed off a couple of his precious bullets at Colclough, then sprinted towards where Tournier lay.

Colclough responded with just one shot, followed by a loud bellow: 'You running scared, Harding?'

Harding ignored the taunt, being too concerned with the contents of Tournier's gun belt. To his relief, it had plenty of slugs. He rolled the body over, unbuckled the belt and dragged it off. Taking some slugs to reload his guns, he then tied the belt around his own waist.

Hearing no sound of movement, he glanced briefly around the rock to see what Colclough was up to. Harding cursed and closed his eyes as another shot crashed into the boulder, showering him with dust and splinters.

He had all the slugs he needed now, but was trapped. If he moved, Colclough would simply gun him down, because Colclough had no distractions now, all his efforts being concentrated on Harding rather than Tournier, Sarah and his own side-kicks.

Harding suddenly hit on a plan to get himself out of the trap he was in. Hauling Tournier's body close to him, he propped it upright against the rock. All he needed to do was distract Colclough for a couple of seconds. That would give him time to escape and return to where he had taken cover before, which was a far better vantage point from which to smoke Colclough out.

Grabbing Tournier's body, he eased it towards the edge of the rock. With a powerful shove, he launched it out into the open. Two shots immediately rang out, one thudding into the already lifeless body and the other causing a cloud of dust to spurt up inches from its feet.

The second Harding heard the crack of the first shot, he staggered out from the opposite side of the rock, trying to block out the pain that still enveloped his body. He dived for cover, managing to grin with pleasure at the thought that he had fooled the other man.

Wiping the sweat from his face, he closed his eyes and tried to figure out what to do next. The anger and disgust at what Colclough had done to Sarah still tasted bitter in his mouth. He wanted to charge straight at him, as he had done to one of his men. But Harding's instincts told him that Colclough wouldn't be panicked as easily as his henchmen. The lawman had been in enough gunfights and taken enough risks to know that he had to keep his head. If Harding charged, Colclough would calmly take aim and pick him off. So Harding waited patiently for his opponent to make the next move.

Suddenly, a single shot echoed through the still air. Puzzled, Harding peered cautiously over the rock. He saw Colclough lying on the ground. Stunned, Harding broke cover and headed straight for him, both guns fully loaded and pointing directly at Colclough's head.

Colclough groaned. A large damp patch of blood had appeared on his left shoulder indicating where the bullet had whacked into him.

'I'll tell you exactly what happened.' At the sound of the voice behind him, Harding spun around. He saw the henchman Colclough had shot walking unsteadily towards him, a smoking gun hanging limply from his hand. 'But I had to get him first so he wouldn't cause me any trouble.'

Harding looked at the man. He recognized him as one of Jenkins' cowhands. 'I know what happened,' Harding replied calmly. 'But you can correct me on any details I might get wrong when I tell the marshal.

The man nodded. 'I was just following orders,' he stammered nervously. 'I was forced to do things I didn't want by threats . . . and I never killed nobody.'

'Don't believe him,' moaned Colclough, his face etched with pain and streaming with sweat. 'He's a liar.'

'You'll have to tell your story to the marshal,' Harding snarled, looking in contempt at the man who had gunned down the woman he had thought might be his wife.

Harding turned to the cowhand. 'Tie him up and help me get the bodies to the horses so we can get them to town.'

When they rode into Sentenas, accompanied by three horses, one carrying the wounded Colclough, the others laden with the bodies of Tournier and Sarah Jenson, Harding headed straight for the sheriff's office.

The marshal was waiting for him. After ordering that all the bodies be laid out in the back, Harding turned to one of the men milling around the office. 'Get a doctor to have a look at him,' Harding said, indicating Colclough. 'He'll need to be healthy for the trial. Then I'll lock him up.'

'From all I've heard, Harding,' the marshal said, 'you should be the one locked up because of all the killing you've done. And you'd better get the doc to have a look at you. You're in one hell of a mess.'

'The only killing I've done is to protect myself. It's your own lawman who's been the cause of the murders, not me. And as for this,' he continued, looking down at his hands, 'I'll get them seen to when we've concluded this business.'

'What do you mean . . . my own lawman?' the marshal asked.

Harding was exhausted. He needed

something to drink. 'Mind if I have some coffee?'

'Nope. Help yourself.'

Harding took a long swig of coffee. 'Colclough was on Jenkins' payroll,' he began. 'That's why the sheriff could never catch any thieves and killers. Because Colclough told Jenkins everything that was going on.'

The marshal's eyebrows shot up but he said nothing.

Harding continued. 'But when Colclough told him that the sheriff was getting real close to putting together some evidence on him, Jenkins decided he had to act. He had killed my brother, to force him off the land he wanted to expand his own holdings, then tried to scare me off. When that didn't work, he tried to kill me as well. But then Colclough's news made him decide to forget me temporarily to kill the sheriff.'

Harding took another swig of coffee. 'It was Ritter who kidnapped the girl, but I don't suppose Jenkins was too happy about that. He probably wanted her killed too. Then Ritter turned on Jenkins and killed him to get his money, not knowing that Jenkins kept it with his lawyer, Jenson. It was Ritter who killed Jenson, whilst trying to rob him.'

Harding placed the mug of coffee on the edge of the desk. 'Then later that night he recruited Tournier at the local cathouse to get rid of me, knowing that I'd be after him for kidnapping the girl. But there's no honour among thieves. Tournier shot Ritter in front of my eyes and took all the money Ritter had stolen. He took the girl to make sure he'd have safe passage to the border.'

Harding picked up the mug of coffee and drained it. 'Now Colclough was real worried when the sheriff was murdered. You see, he needed me as the killer to pin the sheriff's murder on. There was no way he could arrest Jenkins because he was in the man's pay. Then events took a nasty turn for him. I had told him about Tournier and, with the deaths of both Jenkins and Ritter, he knew he'd be exposed if Ritter had told Tournier anything about his involvement with Jenkins. He had to kill Tournier because he was the only person who could condemn him and confirm my innocence.'

Harding's voice broke slightly at the memory as he continued. 'And Colclough had to kill Sarah in case Tournier had mentioned anything to her. Then, with all of them out of the way, he could take me either dead or alive and blame the killings on me. He'd still be deputy . . . despite his hands being stained with blood.'

The marshal eyed Harding. 'You're right.'

'You believe me?'

The marshal nodded. 'When we went through the clothes of the man you shot in the alleyway — Carver — we found this.' The marshal handed Harding a scrap of paper. It read: *Arriving on the Tuesday train. Give Colclough my regards. Tournier.*

'Colclough gave Carver the name of

the killer to get rid of you,' the marshal went on. 'He probably couldn't believe his luck that somebody else, apart from Jenkins, wanted you dead. Jenkins would benefit from your death and he'd have no part of it. Much safer from Colclough's point of view. Only trouble was, Carver wanted things done too quickly and tried to take you himself rather than wait for Tournier.'

'You seem to know a lot about this,' Harding said.

The marshal smiled. 'Remember the cathouse you went to? Well, one of the girls has talked. Told me all about Ritter and Tournier ... but by that time Colclough was after you. Even if he'd killed you, I'd have grilled him until he cracked.'

Harding nodded. 'Are you going to tell Mrs Jenson?' he asked quietly, looking towards the back of the room where Sarah was laid out.

'Yup. By the way, she's paying a reward for the capture of her husband's murderer and daughter's kidnapper.

Looks like it's all yours.'

'Not something I was looking for but maybe it'll help me rebuild my ranch and buy some more stock.' An expression of sadness flitted across his face. 'So long, Marshal.'

As Harding rode out of town, he glanced back once. Maybe he would be happy here some day. But he knew that the memory of Sarah Jenson would take a long time to fade.

THE END

We do hope that you have enjoyed reading this large print book.

Did you know that all of our titles are available for purchase?

We publish a wide range of high quality large print books including:
Romances, Mysteries, Classics
General Fiction
Non Fiction and Westerns

Special interest titles available in large print are:
The Little Oxford Dictionary
Music Book, Song Book
Hymn Book, Service Book

Also available from us courtesy of Oxford University Press:
Young Readers' Dictionary
(large print edition)
Young Readers' Thesaurus
(large print edition)

For further information or a free brochure, please contact us at:
Ulverscroft Large Print Books Ltd.,
The Green, Bradgate Road, Anstey,
Leicester, LE7 7FU, England.
Tel: (00 44) **0116 236 4325**
Fax: (00 44) **0116 234 0205**

Other titles in the
Linford Western Library:

A TOWN CALLED TROUBLESOME

John Dyson

Matt Matthews had carved his ranch out of the wild Wyoming frontier. But he had his troubles. The big blow of '86 was catastrophic, with dead beeves littering the plains, and the oncoming winter presaged worse. On top of this, a gang of desperadoes had moved into the Snake River valley, killing, raping and rustling. All Matt can do is to take on the killers single-handed. But will he escape the hail of lead?

THE WIND WAGON

Troy Howard

Sheriff Al Corning was as tough as they came and with his four seasoned deputies he kept the peace in Laramie — at least until the squatters came. To fend off starvation, the settlers took some cattle off the cowmen, including Jonas Lefler. A hard, unforgiving man, Lefler retaliated with lynchings. Things got worse when one of the squatters revealed he was a former Texas lawman — and no mean shooter. Could Sheriff Corning prevent further bloodshed?

CABEL

Paul K. McAfee

Josh Cabel returned home from the Civil War to find his family all murdered by rioting members of Quantrill's band. The hunt for the killers led Josh to Colorado City where, after months of searching, he finally settled down to work on a ranch nearby. He saved the life of an Indian, who led him to a cache of weapons waiting for Sitting Bull's attack on the Whites. His involvement threw Cabel into grave danger. When the final confrontation came, who had the fastest — and deadlier — draw?

McKINNEY'S LAW

Mike Stotter

McKinney didn't count on coming across a dead body in the middle of Texas. He was about to become involved in an ever-deepening mystery. The renegade Comanche warrior, Black Eagle, was on the loose, creating havoc; he didn't appear in McKinney's plans at all, not until the Comanche forced himself into his life. The US Army gave McKinney some relief to his problems, but it also added to them, and with two old friends McKinney set about bringing justice through his own law.

BLACK RIVER

Adam Wright

John Dyer has come to the insignificant little town of Black River to destroy the last living reminder of his dark past. He has come to kill. Jack Hart is determined to stop him. Only he knows the terrible truth that has driven Dyer here, and he knows that only he can beat Dyer in a gunfight. Ex-lawman Brad Harris is after Dyer too — to avenge his family. The stage is set for madness, death and vengeance.